# I LOVED THE MOTHMAN AND OTHER STORIES

CARI DUBIEL

DUSKBOUND BOOKS

# INTRODUCTION

I always thought cryptids were kind of dumb. A few of my coworkers were really into them, and I think we even had a cryptozoology program at the library where I work. I didn't know a whole lot beyond that, and I had zero belief that the creatures existed, so I never thought much of them. I still don't believe they exist, but I never realized how much they captivate the American mind.

The title story was inspired by our trip to the Mothman Museum in Point Pleasant, West Virginia. We were on our way home from a trip to Pigeon Forge, Tennessee, and we figured the stop would be a fun diversion. We laughed at the shiny Mothman statue and the cryptid references in the small town. Once we entered the museum, though, I started to peruse the many old newspaper articles that lined the walls. And I read. And read. And read.

Mothman entered the national conversation after several people spotted a huge winged creature in the "TNT area" of Point Pleasant. This was a WWII-era bunker site, but Mothman wasn't sighted until the late sixties. After multiple accounts, stories began appearing in the papers, which the Mothman Museum collects. The town's Harris Steakhouse was even rechristened the Mothman Diner, which is recreated inside the museum.

The Silver Bridge, the major route from Point Pleasant over the Ohio River to Gallipolis, Ohio, collapsed in December 1967. The Mothman was never spotted again, and rumors circulated that he had predicted the bridge's untimely destruction. A long-suffering scientist, Robert L. Smith, posited that the sightings were of a sandhill crane, which sports dark wings and red eyes. I recently saw a related crane at my local zoo and could definitely see where the professor was coming from.

This was the first time I had become fascinated with a cryptid. Well, I can't say Mothman invaded my dreams, but I was inspired. I started looking up other cryptids and found that many were steeped in lore. I found a treasure trove of information about Kirtland, Ohio, a town near my childhood home. As a bored teenager, I'd spent years following the Lundgren murder case, where a maniacal cult leader killed a family of his constituents because they could not follow his orders. When I found that the Kirtland Melonheads were associated with the murders —both cursed by Joseph Smith when he went through town in 1833—I couldn't believe it. I went down many rabbit holes of this nature as I wrote these stories. You can read the Appendix to find out more once you've read the stories.

I think I've figured out why cryptids are such a riveting topic. They're modern-day legends, built with history and secrecy. No one can truly prove their existence, yet they exist in our collective mythology. Most importantly, they reveal truths about humans and what we believe. They represent our desires and what we will never be.

A few brief content warnings:

"Curves" includes a creature similar to Cthulhu from Lovecraft's tales. While I recognize their impact on literature and society, I find Lovecraft's intrinsic beliefs problematic. I haven't figured out what to call this monster, though. "Curves" also includes body dysmorphia issues and emotional disturbance.

"Devil Thirteen" includes sexual assault, coercion, and reproductive loss. This is the most difficult story in the collection. Please take care if you are sensitive to any of these themes.

Thank you for reading these stories. They were a blast to write, and I hope you will enjoy the ride too.

-Cari Dubiel
	May 12, 2024

# I LOVED THE MOTHMAN

It's true that when I rolled up to the curb in Point Pleasant, West Virginia, I was unimpressed. That won't be a surprise if you know who I am. It was a slapdash town on the spot where the Ohio and Kanawha Rivers meet. Always wanting to be an important port city but never quite making it. Cursed by the death of Shawnee chief Cornstalk in the 18th century. Maybe that's why the Mothman chose it.

The main street was lined with brick facades and empty buildings. A historic hotel sat across from the Mothman Museum, trying and failing to bring prestige back to the town. The rest of it was all chain restaurants and gas stations, broken cars and pawn shops. Not exactly a prime location for an on-site reporting job.

If you've read the original story, you'll know that my editor sent me there in 2006 for the 40th anniversary of the first Mothman sighting. The museum had just opened, and she wanted me to report on it specifically. I failed to understand how our startup online paper would make any money on such a feature–the Internet was a new frontier, and everyone had a blog.

So I'll cry mea culpa on that one. I'd had no idea how my story would be received.

But we'll get to that.

On a brisk day in October, I stepped out of my silvery Civic and headed toward the museum.

Terri had sent me specifically because, out of our reporters, I lived the closest. Still, it had been a long drive from Akron, and I was happy to stretch my legs. The air had the same character as it did back home: cool but not uncomfortable, a nip on my skin.

Tightening my green patterned scarf around my neck, I pulled open the metal doors. The place was small, a converted storefront, and I wondered what exactly about it was so compelling. I turned in a circle, taking in the Mothman merchandise and apparel filling the room.

"You must be Jenn." The man behind the shop counter rose to greet me. I'd spoken to him regarding the visit.

I stretched out my hand. "And you're Andrew?"

"The very same."

Andrew's voice was familiar but different in person. More bass. He was swarthy, olive skin, big-shouldered but lean through the middle. Bald pate with some dark stubble. But the eyes: they were magnetic. The kind of eyes one might describe in a cheesy romance novel as pools of ink.

Point Pleasant had gotten a lot more interesting.

His hand was warm on mine, the touch fleeting. When I let it go, I cleared my throat, willing my skin to stay unflushed. "I appreciate your time today."

"Not a problem at all. I like to see people like you come in."

*People like me?* Journalists? Ohioans? Pudgy white women? "I hope that's a compliment," I said.

He didn't reply, just whisked aside a curtain made of black plastic vines.

Andrew explained the legend as I goggled at Mothman re-creations. Sculptures, paintings, line drawings. The Mothman was actually quite beautiful, with its strong gray–or black–torso and spread of giant wings. The common denominator: its eyes were always red.

I shifted my focus back to Andrew. He was still talking, even though I'd missed half of what he'd said.

The legend began when Point Pleasant residents sighted a great beast haunting a former World War II munitions plant, now known as the "TNT area" in a local nature preserve. The Mothman was a bad omen, sending the town into a panicked tizzy. Thirteen months later, the Silver Bridge across the river collapsed, killing 46 and injuring many more.

The fervor would have died if not for John Keel, who wrote *The Mothman Prophecies*. He claimed the Mothman was sending him secret messages—when he wasn't making up stories about UFOs and other mysterious happenings. Soon, the town had turned into a Mothman shrine, with a diner for enthusiasts and a local columnist who kept the cryptid alive.

It was all too much exposition for me. I dug my steno pad out of my messenger bag and began scribbling. I stopped to shake out my cramped wrist, and Andrew laughed. "You got enough material yet?"

"I'm getting pictures next." I put the notebook away and searched for my camera. My cheeks flamed, finally getting the better of me.

"It is a lot." Andrew stood by while I began snapping. "Where you going next?"

"The university." It was hard to focus on the conversation and shooting simultaneously. "I've got a meeting with a professor there."

Andrew made a face. "Sandhill Crane guy."

I lowered my camera and raised an eyebrow.

"He'll tell you the Mothman doesn't exist." Andrew pointed to a yellowed article in one of the archival cases. "This one prof kept insisting it was a sandhill crane. They have red around their eyes and it's a big wingspan."

"It's logical."

"And entirely untrue." Andrew ushered me back outside to the main shop. "Come back and I'll show you the reality."

Then I was back on the sidewalk, a breeze chilling me. I pulled my short trench closer and wondered why I felt so alone.

❧

THAT AFTERNOON, I drove more than two hours to the University of West Virginia campus. I met Professor Gordon Smith at a coffee shop there. I was starving, having skipped lunch, but I could grab dinner after the interview before driving back to the hotel.

Smith sat at a long oak table in front of the barista station, sipping from a lidded paper cup. He was tall and spindly, pale, with long fingers and a shock of graying brown hair. I placed him at fifty-ish. "I'm not the professor quoted in the articles," he told me right away. "We were colleagues. Smith is a common name."

I resisted the urge to roll my eyes. "So you followed in his footsteps?"

"Not really. He was in a different department."

"And what's your area of expertise?"

"Anthropology." He tugged on the sleeve of his blue-checked shirt. As he turned his head, I noticed how sharp his cheekbones were. "I do all the interviews Robert used to."

I flipped my steno pad onto the table and started writing. "Why is that?"

"Someone has to do it."

*Someone?* No one else in the area was skeptical about the Mothman? Surely another authority could step up for the task. "What did you learn from Dr. Smith?"

Smith folded his arms. Behind him was a tall shelf filled with books floor to ceiling, probably meant for the shop's guests. The scent of old pages mixed with that of fresh coffee.

"Dr. Smith knew the truth. The so-called Mothman was a sandhill crane."

"I've heard." I planned to look at pictures of the bird as soon as I could get to the public library. Not many places had wi-fi in those days. "He built a strong case."

"Which no one ever paid attention to." Smith practically snarled. Heads twirled in his direction, looks of disgust crossing faces. I flinched. "He was quoted so many times, but no one ever listened. They were too absorbed in their own fantasy."

Despite my trepidation at angering more patrons, I continued. "But why not let them have that? Was it hurting anyone?"

"It was hard for Robert." Gordon Smith's eyes flashed. "He was tired when I met him. He had the knowledge, the experience, and he was ignored. Would you like it if your experience was passed over for a fantasy?"

I inched my chair back. "Not at all."

"So give him that. In your story." He got up, showing off his full height. "Give him the credit he deserves."

IT WAS LATE when I finally checked into the Lowe Hotel. Despite the dreary neighborhood, it was a lovely building. Dated but charming, heavy with history. And rumored to be haunted—par for the course in cursed Point Pleasant.

It was too bad I couldn't stay there longer. But I couldn't expense lodging for more than a night. I could research the rest of the story from home. I'd probably have to visit Andrew again before I left, though. Pitting him psychologically against the professor's words would bring conflict to the piece.

Well. I wouldn't mind having another excuse to see him.

I was about to put on my pajamas when my phone rang. I was tempted to ignore it, but in case it was my mom or roommate checking in, I caved.

Andrew's name showed up on the gray pixelated screen. A shot of adrenaline went through me, but I finally gathered the nerve to answer. Maybe he remembered something I could use.

"You up for an adventure?" he asked with no preamble.

"Depends what kind."

"Let me take you to the TNT area."

I sucked in a breath. "The actual…"

"You know it." I could sense the grin in his tone.

"At night?"

"It's the only way to have an authentic experience."

I peered out the window. The sky was black. And I was hungry—I never did get dinner, opting to move as fast as I could away from Gordon Smith and UWV.

"Take you to Taco Bell first? Show you the finest cuisine in Point Pleasant. Well, Gallipolis."

My heart sped up. "Sure. Yeah."

"Pick you up in ten."

He hung up. I stared at the wallpaper for a moment, letting my thoughts drift. This would be good for my story. And I couldn't deny the attraction between us... unless I was imagining it.

Could I trust Andrew, though? I thought so. I had mace in my purse, at least.

I went outside to meet him as promised, clutching my favorite fuzzy blanket in case it got cold. The silver Mothman statue across from the hotel loomed ominous in the moonlight.

Andrew drove up in a clanking Buick Century and rolled down his window. "Please enter my chariot, dear princess."

"You mean queen?" I had to pull hard to get the door open. The car smelled musty and vaguely smoky.

"I don't smoke." He must have read my expression. "Inherited it when my dad died."

I ran my hand along the fuzzy gray seat. "I'm so sorry."

"It's fine. It was a few years ago, but I can't seem to get the smell out."

He paused, some memory passing over his face. Then he put the car in gear, and we headed out.

After a decadent meal of a Crunchwrap Supreme and a few gorditas, we were back on the road. We didn't talk much. The wildlife preserve was huge, and Andrew searched a while for an entrance. Eventually, he found a dirt access road, and we followed the bumpy terrain as far as the Buick could go.

He put the car in park and killed the engine, then produced a flashlight from under his seat. The light bobbed in the dark as he went around the car to let me out. I grasped his hand without a word.

We assessed the area. Bunkers from wartime hulked around us, ominous silhouettes. I'd read that there were still live bombs here.

"Has anyone seen him recently?" I asked.

"A few people have said so." He gestured to the land. "Camping's not allowed here, but people sneak in."

I blinked. The night was getting cold. I wrapped my blanket around me and hugged myself around the waist. "Are you sure it wasn't a sandhill crane?"

"I'm sure."

"Why?"

He moved the light in silent circles. "The legend gives me something to live for. Without it, I'm a meaningless dude shilling T-shirts."

I felt a rush of empathy. Despite what he said, I knew Andrew had a purpose. I didn't. I floated from job to job, landing on the ridiculous blog site that would never make me money. Well, it eventually brought in the cash, but I didn't know that at the time.

I inched toward him and put my hand on his arm. It was heavy, muscular. He smelled of sandalwood and vanilla.

Andrew dropped the flashlight.

As I reached for his mouth, cupping his cheeks in my palms, I saw a flash of red in his eyes.

My arms went to his strong back. I traced the wings beneath his T-shirt. I breathed in, taking in all of him. Who he really was.

"Is this okay?" he asked.

"Yes."

"You aren't scared?"

I was. But I wanted him.

Andrew's shirt tore. The fabric shredded under my hands. The wings emerged, spanning wide, engulfing me.

BACK AT THE HOTEL, I woke dazed, sure I'd dreamed it. My head pounded as if I had a hangover, but I hadn't drunk a drop.

I had enough for the story. I should have headed home right then. But his pull was magnetic, like his eyes. I couldn't leave yet.

Once I got ready and checked out, I found my car and stuffed my suitcase in the trunk. The Mothman statue blinded me, sunlight reflecting off the metal.

As I wandered the banks of the Ohio River, I watched the water roll by. I came across a plaque honoring the victims of the bridge collapse, and I winced. I hadn't written nearly enough about the disaster. I would have to go back to the car for my camera.

I doubled back to the main street, eyeballing my little silver coupe, and ran smack into a wall of a man.

"Hi, Jenn." Andrew jingled the keys to the museum doors. "What brings you here? I thought you were headed home."

My stomach dropped. I decided to play it cool even though my mouth was dry, my palms sweating. "Just a few more things to do before I wrap things up."

He thumbed back toward the coffee shop in the next storefront. "Want to get coffee? On me."

I didn't need a stimulant. I was already shaking. But I went with him.

When we reached the shop, Andrew stepped to the counter. I studied the rippling muscles on his back, the blue T-shirt stretching across them. No outline of wings.

Maybe I did dream the entire thing.

He handed me a cappuccino, even though I didn't order one. Then he pulled out my chair.

"I'm not going to lie, Jenn." Andrew leaned forward over his own coffee. "I wish you weren't leaving."

I thought of my dingy apartment, its ugly carpeting, the stains on its beige walls. "I'm not really tied to anything in Akron. I could stay."

"Might be a rash decision. But I could at least take you on a date. Besides this one. If you consider this a date." His face flushed. "I'd like to get to know you better."

"You certainly did last night."

He froze. "Um... what?"

My stomach twisted, but I recovered. "I mean, sorry, I was being too forward. I, uh, dreamed about you last night."

Andrew blinked. "Wow. Well, uh, that's cool."

I'd freaked him out.

He wasn't the Andrew of last night. Not even close.

"Maybe we could set something up for real," he mumbled. "Give me your number?"

I tugged a business card out of my purse and handed it to him. He pocketed it and stood. "I have to get back from the store, but..." The smile returned, if briefly, and I felt a streak of hope. "Let's talk."

After Andrew left, I stayed in the coffee shop. Again, I had the feeling that I should have left right then. But instead, I pulled my laptop from my messenger bag and opened a Word document. I ordered another cappuccino, even if I didn't need it, and stared at the blank screen.

The cafe had a "Mothman Special" dessert. Oreo ice cream with two red cherries on top. I ordered that too. The hard chair felt more and more uncomfortable. Just like me. Point Pleasant was telling me to leave.

I forced myself to I pack my things. I was about to head out when I caught movement outside the window.

I wasn't the only one who noticed. People rushed to look out, crowding the front of the store. Some stepped outside—others put their hands on the glass, transfixed.

"I don't believe it," someone said. "In broad daylight?"

A grayish black creature stalked down the sidewalk, grumbling and moaning. The sounds were unearthly. My insides pinched. This couldn't be the creature. He wasn't like that.

As it got closer, I saw it wasn't the Mothman. Not even close. It was tall, at least six feet and likely more. The feathers lining its costume ruffled in the breeze. The mask's eyes weren't red, although they were graced with red and white accents. The wings expanded, and a long beak extended as the person tilted up their head.

"It was a sandhill crane!" squawked Gordon Smith.

FINALLY, I prepared to leave Point Pleasant. I shoved my messenger bag and purse onto the seat, got in the car, started it up. But an odd feeling nagged at me like an itch I couldn't scratch. I couldn't leave yet.

We didn't have GPS in 2006, so I stopped in the local library and printed out a MapQuest. I backtracked to the Taco Bell in Gallipolis, got another Crunchwrap with a couple of tacos, and sucked down a Baja Blast as I drove toward the wildlife preserve. I searched for a while until I came across the same access road, easier to see in the daylight.

I ate my food, snapped some more photos, then sat under a tree till dusk. It was warmer today, but once the sun went down, I was chilled again. As I watched the sunset, resplendent in pinks and purples, I pulled my hoodie on and wrapped my blanket around my shoulders.

The sky darkened. The moon came out. Stars.

Beyond the tree, I caught it. A flap of wings. The sound leathery against the empty night.

He soared down, not bothering to hide his true form. I took him in: bald head, dark wings, red eyes glimmering.

"You came," I said.

"Why wouldn't I?" His voice didn't carry the same weight as Andrew's. It was soft, buttery.

I shrugged even though I was shaking. "I don't know."

He moved closer. This time he smelled of the woods: tree bark, plants, earth. "I'm glad you came back."

"I'm leaving."

"I know."

"You could come with me." I slapped my hand across my mouth, regretting the sentence as soon as I spoke it.

My invitation didn't faze him. "You know I can't."

I reached for his rough palm. "I won't forget you."

He responded by coming closer. And again, he folded his wings around me.

I WENT HOME and told my roommate I needed a place of my own. I applied for full-time jobs, positions that would provide benefits and a regular salary. Health insurance was like gold. I got a gig designing ads for a magazine that catered to home shoppers. The products were funny gadgets that I could never imagine buying. Automatic cat boxes, full-body copper sleeves, poorly made back massagers. Onesie pajamas for the whole family. My paycheck came every two weeks, and I found a decent apartment with a balcony where I could watch the sun set.

I continued writing for Terri. The job was better as a side gig—I wasn't scraping the barrel for cash anymore. She e-mailed me upon reading my first draft. *WTF happened down there?*

We published it. It went viral before viral was a thing. I ignored all the nasty comments as the money rolled into my bank account. I felt like a queen in a treasure trove, preening atop my mountain of gold.

Everything was good. Except that one small thing.

I'm going there this weekend. It's the 50th anniversary now—a big deal. Terri asked me to write a follow-up. She works for BuzzFeed now. I'm more than happy to do it. Andrew and I are still in touch, although we never dated. I haven't dated anyone since that night in the field. But I hope Andrew and I will grab coffee under less awkward circumstances.

I will stay in the Lowe again and walk the river. Pay respects to the dead. In the museum, there will be more portraits of him, more artistic renderings.

I've stayed away from the wildlife preserve. It's still possible I dreamed those nights, and I've been scared of what might happen if I returned. When I went back to Ohio ten years ago, I wanted to start a new life, and I did it. I'm proud of that.

But tonight, I'm stopping at Taco Bell, and I'm going to the woods.

# GREG FROM ACCOUNTING

**Sunday Night**

She hates this job more than she's ever hated anything before.

Greg's desk is always dirty. Misha from Facilities sighs as she pulls out his chair and vacuums underneath it. These entitled people, leaving their empty wrappers on their keyboards, coffee moldering in mugs. It is not her job to clean up after them, only to empty their trash, vacuum, and dust. But Misha can't let those messes sit, and now she's spoiled those inconsiderate jerks.

But Greg. There's always sand under his desk. Does he go to the beach every day? Misha is new to town, so she could be wrong, but she doesn't know of a beach anywhere near here. She is confused, but she doesn't ask questions.

Misha daydreams of a new life, one where she's not relegated to night cleaning duty, where she's the owner of this cubicle instead of just passing through. What does Greg have that she doesn't? A messy set of shoes, a propensity for sloth?

She knows there are cameras in here. She knows she shouldn't snoop. But the sand is coming out from below his desk drawers, she reasons. She needs to clean that up. His cube is an eyesore.

Misha yanks the drawer open. It is filled to the brim with sand.

Well, this explains where he gets it.

But the why is still lodged in Misha's mind. Something is wrong with his man—she's never met him, but she's been suspicious from the beginning. He has no pictures on his desk. No family, no dog. He has no trash can. She keeps bringing one over from a different cube, but it's always gone the next night. No place to put those goddamn candy wrappers.

She sinks her hand into the sand and filters it through her fingers. It does feel good, just a bit gritty, mostly smooth and white. Not like beach sand. She's never been to a desert, but she imagines that sand is like this. Misha looks down just as a creature pops its head out of the pile.

She yelps and draws her hand back. "What the fuck!"

The creature is small but terrifying. It has no eyes, only a huge gaping maw of teeth. It's snapping at her, reaching as if her fingers were still within reach. It makes a horrible high-pitched noise, somewhere between a howl and a chitter.

Misha shoves the drawer shut. She's breathing hard, backing away from the desk. She needs to tell her supervisor she's never going near Greg from Accounting's cubicle ever again.

## Monday Morning

The thing about IT is that the employees go everywhere. Sure, they sometimes hole themselves in their offices and solve tickets remotely. But hardware isn't going to replace itself, and Matt from IT is eager to walk the floor.

Matt's an extrovert. He struts. He does it purposefully, his shoulders bouncing as he strolls through the hallways of Braggerton. He prides himself on being available whenever someone needs him, his phone on vibrate in his back pocket, ready to jump on the elevator or call someone at their Denver location. He always exceeds expectations on his reviews. Work is the best part of his day.

Today he's dressed in a blue collared shirt, a patterned tie, and pressed khakis. Matt makes it a point to dress well every day. Does he get dirty on the floor under the computers? Sure. Does he flip his tie over his shoulder like a badass? Always.

He's been summoned to Accounting to look at a malfunctioning computer. Peg, the Head of Accounting, ushers him into the department. She's white, in her mid-fifties, with graying hair and a neck that betrays her age. "Thanks for coming down, Matt," she says.

"Anytime, Peg!" He flashes his thousand-watt smile. "You know how much I love helping you."

Her smile back is not so enthusiastic. "Well, you can help me with this computer. Greg is out of town, and there's a mess."

Matt trails her to Greg from Accounting's cubicle. The first thing he sees is sand all over the floor. "What happened here?" he asks, circling the mess. It looks like someone went to the beach and shook off their flip-flops.

Peg shrugs. "Who knows? Greg is a bit odd."

"You said he was out of town, though?"

"He left Friday."

Matt nods and squats down, trying not to get dirty. He quickly learns that this is a futile exercise when he loses his balance and fine white grains coat his knees. But he is determined, and he'll embrace the mess and get down to business.

Matt presses the power button, but the computer doesn't boot. "If he wasn't here, how did you find out this station wasn't working?"

Somewhere from above him, Peg says, "Misha from Facilities reported the mess. She said he had a drawer full of sand. And that there were creatures living in it."

"Huh." Matt thinks about this as he scoots the computer across the carpet. He shimmies out from under the desk and picks up the PC. He really needs to talk to Bob, the Head of IT, about the locations of these stations. They shouldn't be on the floor. Someone could easily trip themselves or knock down a tower. And those things ain't cheap.

He bangs his leg on the drawer as he gets up, but he grits his teeth and doesn't swear. Cursing would not be a good look for the IT Department. Matt must always be on his best behavior.

He places the PC on the desk and leans over. "Can I open the drawer?"

Peg shrugs again. "Be my guest."

Matt tugs on the silver handle, and the drawer slides out. It's deep, meant for hanging files, but there are none inside. Instead, there is more sand, gritty along the smooth bottom of the drawer.

He shakes his head. This isn't what he was tasked to do. He needs to refocus.

Matt pulls his screwdriver from his pocket and gets to work on the sides of the case. A swooshing sound is coming from the interior, and he gets a bad feeling, but he already has the plastic back open.

Sand pours from the computer onto the floor. Onto Matt. The fine grains are inside his shirt, in his pants. He lets out a groan, then slaps his sand-covered hand onto his sand-covered mouth. Another groan, and he realizes he's not going to save this encounter. Peg is seeing him vulnerable.

There is sand all over the floor, coating it. "I'm sorry, Peg," Matt says.

She waves a hand. "I'll call Facilities."

"No, no. I insist. I'll bring the vacuum up, and then we'll get you a new PC lickety-split."

"It's okay, Matt. I don't even know when Greg will be back."

Peg sighs and turns away as if she'd never wanted to ask him there in the first place.

It's too hard to explain to Bob, so Matt keeps his head down until it's time to head home. He works on tickets and remotes into people's computers to adjust their software. It's technically not his job—he's a hardware guy—but they always have a backlog, so he's sure Bob will be fine with it. The sand itches–it's everywhere–but he needs to stick it through the day. He can provide excellent customer service, even if it's over the phone or online.

His pants are wedged into his crotch by the time he gets to the car. The insides of his thighs are scratchy, not to mention the sensitive areas. Matt is more depressed than usual as he starts the long drive home.

He lives in Kent, the college town he never left, but works on the east side of Cleveland. His house is not his—he rents—and his apartment is above the loudest fraternity he's ever heard. They lease the apartment so they can make extra money for the brotherhood. Matt's looking for a new place. For now, he waddles up the back stairs and heads straight to the bathroom.

The shower is warm along his back and body. He washes everything. It feels like a baptism, the sand sluicing off him almost holy.

Matt gets out of the shower and wraps a fluffy towel around himself. He always buys fluffy towels. They get him energized about the day ahead. He rarely showers after work, but he regrets nothing. He feels good. Refreshed. Happy enough to make the chicken parm he'd bought ingredients for. He always buys meat for meal prep but never eats it.

Normally, when night falls, Matt begins to fade. Darkness creeps in, covers him. It's like suffocating. His sunny personality wanes away until all that's left is despair. He settles into bed for a pathetic wank and a bowl of ice cream (not at the same time). He drifts off to Netflix feeling empty.

Tonight, it feels easier to fight the beast. He takes a spin on his treadmill. The wank is extra hot. He dusts off a book on business acumen and reads before bed instead of eating ice cream. Maybe this is a spark of hope.

**Two Weeks Later**

It's bright and early on a Monday, and Matt's checking his email. He always arrives one hour before his shift. It gives him time to settle in, to drink the protein shake that starts his day.

He's halfway through a sip when he sees the email from Peg. He'd forgotten about the sand in the computer, the strange desk of Greg from Accounting. The subject line reads *Monday morning—Matt?*

It's a meeting request. Three people are invited: Matt, Greg, and Bob.

Matt's hand shakes on his mouse. Greg is back. Did Matt do something wrong when he was opening the computer? Had he hallucinated the entire thing?

The meeting is scheduled for nine-thirty. Matt makes sure his tie is straight, checks his hair in the mirror. When he sees Bob's door close, he jumps, clamping down on his anxiety. He calls up his golden retriever personality, a different guy from the one who inhabits that scuzzy apartment.

"Good morning!" he says jubilantly.

There are circles under Bob's eyes, carved into his light brown skin. He scrubs a hand over his tight, curly hair and nods at Matt.

Matt sees an opportunity. "Can I get you some coffee, boss?"

It's easier to use familiarities with his superiors. He would feel strange calling them by their first names, but using their last names is too formal.

Bob shakes his head. "C'mon."

Though he can be blunt, sometimes even mean, Bob is a good man. But he's often inscrutable, and Matt nearly vibrates as he worries about this meeting. Have Bob and Peg talked about this? Who is getting in trouble? Greg wasn't even here. Although he did have a buttload of sand inside his computer case.

Finally, in the elevator, he blurts it out. "Am I in trouble?"

Bob turns, brow furrowing. "Huh?"

"This meeting."

"What about it?"

Matt stammers. "It's just, just not... not usual for us to meet with Accounting. Peg didn't leave any information, so I couldn't prepare."

Bob chuckles. The elevator dings, and they step off. Sweat is beading on the back of Matt's neck. He loosens his tie, then re-tightens it.

"You're not in trouble," Bob says. "Just trying to get to the bottom of this."

*The bottom of what?*

∾

THEY ARRIVE at Greg's desk, but Greg is not there. Even so, Bob stops and peers into the cube. "It doesn't look bad. Think Peg's off her rocker?"

Matt is still freaking out. He grits his teeth, and they squeak against each other.

"Off whose rocker?" Peg asks.

She is in front of them, and Matt thanks the gods that he did not respond to Bob. Bob isn't rattled, though. He sticks out his hand, and Peg takes it, serving Bob with a healthy dose of side-eye. Matt shifts from foot to foot beside them like a good peon.

Bob pretends Peg hasn't responded to his comment. "Did you want to meet in the conference room?" he asks her. "I've heard Accounting has great coffee."

Matt tromps behind the two of them. Peg opens the door and lets them both in, and sure enough, the heady scent of good coffee fills the room. Bob goes immediately to the table to fill a paper cup from the urn, but Matt is looking in the center of the room. Looking at Greg.

Matt makes it a point to know everyone in the company, but he's never really examined Greg. Never understood what makes Greg tick.

Greg is disheveled. He wears a coral polo, which doesn't match his ruddy face and soft jaw. His eyebrows are dark brown and overgrown, eyes small and beady like a young Jack Black. Greg's hair is tangled and tousled, also too long.

And the man smells. Matt can't put a finger on exactly what Greg smells like. It's almost a rotting smell, like halitosis, but there's another note of scent. Wind, perhaps, or beach salt. It makes Matt want to throw up. He heads back to the coffee table to pour himself a huge cup. Might mask the odor.

When they are all at the table, Peg folds her hands in front of her. Greg's eyes flit between the three of them.

"We need to talk about company property," she says.

Pieces slot together in Matt's mind. Greg's being held responsible for the damage to the equipment. Of course that's why Matt's here. Because he was the one who discovered it. He sighs, lets out a deep breath. Maybe deeper than it should have been, because Peg and Bob both look at him.

"Sorry," he says. "Frog in my throat. Continue."

Oh God, he's made it worse. Matt resolves not to say anything or do anything else until this meeting is over.

Peg regroups. "Matt, would you please tell Greg what you found?"

So much for not saying anything. "Um, sure."

Matt reiterates what happened that day, casting glances back at Peg to make sure he's telling the story right. He realizes that he never filled out an incident report for Bob. Greg's scent is overpowering. Matt feels hot.

When Matt is finished, Peg turns back to Greg. The man doesn't look nervous or scared. His lips are pursed, and he stares back at his boss with no qualms.

"Can you explain this?" she asks.

Matt is taking little sips of air, all he can get. Bob turns to him with a concerned look, but Matt is not going to mess up this time. He needs to hear what Greg has to say.

Greg shrugs. "It's a hazard of the job."

Peg's stare could kill a worm. "Really."

"Not the accounting job." Greg waves his hand. "Caring for the sandworms."

Did Matt hear him right?

"Greg." Peg squeezes her folded hands tighter. "We've discussed this. The sand in the cube, the long vacations. I'm afraid I can't approve any more. HR has told me I can't grant so much unpaid time off. If the department can get by without you, then we don't need you."

Greg's dark eyes go crossed. "Okay…"

"Misha from Facilities said there were actual worms in your drawer."

"Yeah. I told you. The sandworms."

Matt can tell Bob is as perplexed as he is. But Matt's face is heating with confusion. His stomach is twisting. He has to get up.

"One second, everyone, please excuse me." He holds up one finger before collapsing to the carpet.

MATT'S EYES FLUTTER OPEN. He can't tell where he is. Home? His mother's? She's been gone for so long. He's been alone for so long.

Then there is a looming face, and that smell.

He groans. "Phil? From Accounting?"

"It's Greg."

Right. Matt remembers. The strange dirty man, his boss, and Matt's boss. But the bosses are not there anymore. It's him and Greg.

"You gotta see where I'm coming from, man."

Matt doesn't want this man breathing over his face. He sits up slowly, drawing a hand to his cheek. He needs water. But Greg is lost in his message.

"They're the only friends I've ever had. It's why I have to go back to Mongolia at least once a year. It's best if I can go twice, but you heard what Peg said." He laces his fingers together and wrings his hands. "They'll make it though. I'll find a way to make it work."

Matt's afraid he might pass out again, but then Bob and Peg come running back into the room. Wendy from the clinic is with them, brandishing her stethoscope and a blood pressure cuff. Peg shoos Greg away so Wendy can work her magic. But the nurse just loops the stethoscope over her neck after she's examined Matt.

"Panic attack," Wendy says briskly. "Happens to all of us. Mark—"

"It's Matt," Matt says.

"Matt. Take it easy today, maybe go home early. You shouldn't be this stressed at work. It's not healthy." Wendy mentions the employee assistance program, as she always does, and presses a card into Matt's sweaty palm. "Please contact me if you have more problems, yes?"

He nods, unable to think of any other response.

**Tuesday**

Matt's not in the right mood.

He misses the hope he had that day. When the sand poured out of the computer and he felt some kind of triumph. This morning, he didn't even make it to work at seven like he normally does. Didn't have time to make the protein shake, didn't put on a tie.

Bob asks if he's all right.

Matt shrugs. "Yesterday was rough."

"You're telling me. Can I get you some coffee?"

Proof that Bob is truly a nice person under that hard exterior. Matt knows it. Even if he doesn't drink the coffee, Matt wants his boss to perform the favor. "Absolutely," he says.

Bob is gone a long time. He returns with a hot Styrofoam cup and presses it into Matt's hands. Matt takes a sip and recognizes the flavor from Accounting.

"Yes, I went up there." Bob reads his mind. "I won't lie. I wanted to see what was going on."

Matt shakes his head, rubs his eyes. Moves his keyboard over so the coffee won't spill. "So what is going on?"

Bob leans forward. "You should come upstairs with me. Later on. Past closing."

Matt feels a twisting low in his stomach. "You serious?"

"As a heart attack."

Bob's breath is tinted with coffee. Matt swallows, tries to ignore the waves of air emanating towards him.

"You ever heard about dog energy and cat energy?"

Matt stares. His mind is too bleary to comprehend new information.

Bob holds out his hands, mimicking a scale. He tilts one arm to the side. "Here, we have dog energy. Excitement. Eagerness. A desire to help." Then he moves to the other side, as if weighting it. "Then there's cat energy. Strong indifference, but available to help and comfort when needed."

When Matt doesn't respond, Bob continues. "You've normally got the dog energy, Matt. You're the kind of guy everyone wants to have around. Dogs are universally loved, don't you think? At least the ones who don't bark or jump. Or growl."

Matt reaches for his cup, and the coffee slops forward onto his shirt. It's only a few small drops, but it feels like an emergency. He shoves the cup towards Bob and roots in his top drawer for his Tide stick.

"The dog energy's not there today," Bob says. "You're skittish. Unstable. I think you need a day or two."

The Tide seeps into his shirt, and Matt relaxes a little. He finally has the urge to speak. "Don't think so."

"Well, then, I'll leave you to it." Bob gets up and slaps his hands on his thighs. "Just so you know, I've got cat energy."

Matt gets up too. "Yeah, I can tell."

He gets a call—Bill from Sales. There's a malfunctioning printer on the sixth floor. On the way upstairs, Matt stops at the water fountain and pours the coffee down the drain.

He doesn't need Bob to stay late with him. He doesn't need a chaperone. Besides, he's behind on his work because he was late. He needs to figure out how to get the dog energy back.

Because Bob was right. Matt had spent the day fighting the thought. He was a man, not a mongrel. But as he drifted, the sky outside growing dreary, he felt his energy draining away.

He's in the elevator with Misha from Facilities, and he tries not to stare. She's a beautiful woman of Russian descent, all wan skin and fine blond hair. Her belt is ornamented with a hammer and a measuring tape. "I'm not a cleaner," she says to him, and he nods. "I'm assigned to cleaning today."

"Got it," he rasps. The belt, unfortunately, is sexy.

Misha narrows her eyes at him. "What are you doing up here?"

Matt hesitates but finally grits out a response. "There's a computer up here I need to look at," he tells her as the elevator dings and they step out. "I already replaced it, but I have a bad feeling."

Dave from IT replaced the tower after Matt passed out, but it's close enough.

She leans toward him. The clean citrus scent of her hair is intoxicating. "Is it Greg's from Accounting?"

Shit. Bob had mentioned this yesterday, that Misha was the one to find the sand initially. "Yeah," Matt says. He might as well be honest with her. "I'm afraid things are gonna get worse up there."

"You're telling me." Misha shakes her head. "C'mon."

He trails her. His heart is speeding, both from her proximity and that of Greg's computer. Matt can see it from here, the floor ringed with sand.

Then Misha gasps.

"What?" He leans closer. *Don't be a creeper, don't be a creeper.*

His gaze catches on it. A framed photo on Greg's desk. The man stands in front of the camera, his smile wide and toothy. Behind him is a hulking monster with no eyes, mouth open to a maw of teeth.

"Jesus Christ." Misha crosses herself. "This is where I found them. I don't wanna touch it. I said I was never coming back up here again, but Peg asked me to. I fucking hate these people—what's your name again?"

Matt's mouth is dry as he answers her.

"Matt." Now she jabs her elbow in the direction of the drawer. "You wanna open it?"

He stares, feeling like he's going to his grave.

"They didn't do anything to me last time. They were just... gross. Bizarre. Not the kind of thing you'd see in an office for sure."

"Is Greg gonna get fired?"

Misha shrugs. "Not my problem. Oh, hey, I know I said I fucking hate these people, but not you. Probably sounded like I did before, since I asked for your name. The truth is, I didn't know you, so I couldn't hate you. But I know you now. Don't do anything to fuck that up. Like, maybe open this drawer so I don't have to."

Matt sighs, heavy. He doesn't want Misha on his bad side. He can picture her on his good side. So he lunges for the drawer.

It's empty.

He and Misha trade glances.

She grabs her hammer out of her belt and throws it down on the carpet. It hits with a thud.

But here—here's something.

Sand pouring in front the back of the deep drawer. Like it was trapped somewhere, waiting to be rolled out. Misha roars and grabs Matt's hand, and he lets her do it. She has a death grip.

The monsters surge out too. They're tiny, not like the behemoth pictured with Greg, but maybe scarier on account of their size. They peek out from their sand, jaws snapping. Their skin is as red as blood.

～

## Wednesday

The next day, HR walks Greg out. Matt watches out his window. The man carries one box, and Matt wonders how all that sand could be contained in that tiny cardboard vessel.

It's the end. But it's not.

When Peg calls him, he ignores the phone. Someone else can rip apart that computer. Someone else can be bitten by those sharp teeth. Matt is done with Accounting. He'll focus on Sales. Those guys have big dog energy.

Matt's tired and suspicious. Misha works three to ten, but he isn't sure if he should find her or stay ensconced at his desk. He's in a polo and pants he picked off the floor. Maybe tomorrow he'll try a dress shirt.

It's only been a few days, but he feels the man inside him hiding. That persona was fake all along, he realizes. Concealing this excuse for a human. Someone who deserves nothing special. A lonely existence, eating ramen noodles in front of the TV.

The weather has warmed. The sun is radiating through Matt's window. He will go outside, he decides. The light may put a new shine on him.

He picks up his pace as he strides out of the elevator and through the circling doors to the outside. "My man!" calls out one of the guys from Sales. "Printer wizard!"

Matt summons a smile and a wave. "You know it!"

He sits down on a concrete step. There's a food truck out there shilling hot dogs. Matt reaches in his pocket; his wallet's on his desk. He's not sure if he cares enough to go back upstairs. But the hot dogs are cheap, and they look good.

And Greg, formerly of Accounting, is turning from the line and walking toward him.

Matt jumps to his feet and is about to rush back into the building, but Greg is almost running. "Hey!"

He doesn't have to be nice to Greg. They're no longer colleagues. Hell, Matt barely knew him to begin with, and he certainly hadn't been to the guy's cube before this month. He starts speed-walking, but Greg is too fast and snags his elbow.

"Hey, Matt," Greg says.

Matt sighs and turns, resolved to his fate.

"I wanted to explain. I feel bad."

Greg does look penitent. But Matt doesn't need the apology. He needs to go back to work. The only good part of his day.

Matt shakes his head. "It's fine. I'm fine."

"It's important that you know." Greg holds up the box. "I've been fired from so many jobs. It's not a big deal. You don't have to feel bad for me."

Matt channels Bob. "I know."

Greg holds up a finger and pulls the box lid open. Matt recoils as the little worms escape from it. He glances around, hoping someone will come to his rescue, but no one notices him.

"I go to Mongolia because I love these goddamn things." Tears well in Greg's eyes, but his hands are busy and he can't wipe them away. They streak down his cheeks into his beard and onto his lips.

Matt recoils, but he can't keep his eyes off the creatures.

"They don't live long. I need to go back and visit their mother. You know. I shouldn't have put her picture on my desk. Maybe I could have stayed longer. I'm not bad at finance, you know. They wreck me, Matt. But I need them."

A worm is on the ground now, headed toward Matt. He moves to step on it, but Greg pushes him out of the way. Greg reaches down, and the worm revolves around his finger. With nowhere else to go, the worm clamps down on Greg's arm.

Matt might faint again, or throw up, or both.

"Come on, give it a try." Greg holds out his arm. The creature gently detaches from Greg and slithers onto Matt's before Matt can stop it. He goes stone still as the gaping mouth affixes to his skin.

The horror falls away. Matt watches as the thing moves. He doesn't feel bad, not like the worm is drawing out blood. In fact, he feels good. Big worm energy flowing through him. It's like a drug.

Greg is hesitant. "Now do you see?"

Matt sees. Matt sees everything.

"You wanna go to Mongolia with me sometime?" Greg detaches the worm from Matt's arm, and Matt feels an emptiness where it used to be. The worm coils around Greg's wrist, and Matt watches its long tail move like a snake's.

The sand. The worms. Misha. The Feelings. All of it bleeds before his eyes.

"Go," he says.

Greg's hangdog expression remains for a second, but he follows Matt's direction. Matt watches him retreat, heading back toward the hot dog truck.

There's a spring in his step as he returns to the office. There's a salad waiting for him. Maybe he'll go to the free gym and lift. Or work on the core. These abs don't maintain themselves. He's jaunty, visiting the departments, calling out to see if everyone's okay. There's nothing he can't fix today.

# SASSY

As Sydney's face pressed against the damp forest floor, she realized she should not have attended this party.

She'd collided with the leafy ground after tripping over a huge dead log. Prior to that, she'd been making out with Joey Carmichael, who no longer seemed to be present.

Her cheek stung hot, and when she put a finger to the skin, it was tender. Could she have broken a cheekbone? She'd be homecoming queen this year, and her pictures would come out terrible.

Sydney groaned as she pushed herself to her elbows, then to her feet. Dirt clung to her clothes. She shouldn't have worn her new jumpsuit—too nice for this kind of party, a wild kegger in the woods. Maybe it would wash, although she could always buy another one.

She fished in her pocket for her phone. She'd drop a pin, text Natalia. If she wasn't making out with some guy or girl, she would come get Sydney. She'd surely be stoned and drunk, but at least they'd be together.

The screen lit up—the flashlight worked. But no signal.

"Fuck you, Joey!" she called into the distance.

Her voice reverberated back to her. When she found Joey, she was going to murder him. At least she had time to think about how she'd do it.

Sydney pointed the light at the ground. The air was warm, sticky, wrapped around her like a choking vine. But it wasn't too hot, maybe high seventies. Just humid. She balanced the phone while batting at mosquitoes.

She'd only walked for a little while when dizziness struck her hard. She clamped her eyes shut, fist squeezed around her phone. The force of it almost dropped her again, but she steeled herself to stay upright. *You got this, Ross. You're a warrior.*

Sydney was not a warrior. Her slim body was a result of good genetics. Her mother had already warned her that this would not last. Sydney had briefly considered a diet and exercise routine, but then she started watching TikTok and forgot. "Maybe you could find health tips on there," her mother said, but Sydney was already back on thirst traps by then.

Okay, so she couldn't fight to survive and couldn't communicate with anyone. Awesome. Sydney bit her lip and slowed until the vertigo dissipated and she got her bearings. She forced herself to breathe. Wouldn't Natalia realize Sydney was gone? And how did that fuckhead Joey get back? His phone probably didn't work either…

A low moan emanated from a tree beside her.

Sydney froze.

Could be Joey. Especially if he was hurt. Maybe trying to get her attention. She didn't care. She kept going.

Then it came again. Stronger, louder. She stayed still.

The noise was too loud, too animalistic to be Joey. It had to be a bear—how many other dangerous creatures lived in the forest? Unless a hawk dived down to drag her across the lake to Canada. That was a stretch.

Her muscles were so tight as they strained to stay motionless.

The heat was closing in now. She felt it behind the tree. There was a foul smell she couldn't describe. Like body odor but mixed with rot and soil.

She braced herself and waited.

WHEN SHE WOKE UP, it was morning.

She blinked, clearing the fuzz from her vision. She was still in the woods. The trees formed a canopy that filtered the beating sun. The humidity, though—it pooled under her arms and beaded on her forehead. She must smell as bad as...

The creature. She remembered nothing after feeling it near her—she must have passed out.

Her head hurt. All of her hurt. Her back from sleeping on the ground, her limbs from being curled too tight.

Sydney staggered to her feet and shaded her eyes. She spotted her phone thrown a few feet away and bent to pick it up. Maybe she could find a place with signal. But people had to be looking for her... right?

She'd always been popular. Her honey-blonde hair, natural at that, and impossible body drew people to her before she even spoke. It bothered her sometimes, so she made sure to charm these people. To express her intelligence in any way she could. But that wouldn't help her now. Maybe she didn't matter if she wasn't there to look at.

She laid her palm against the side of her face as the world began to spin.

"Sydney!"

Her mouth was dry. "Here!"

"Sydney!" It was Natalia, coming closer. Natalia, her best friend, ride or die since they were in the second grade. Sydney moved toward the sound, following it like a homing beacon.

Natalia appeared, bursting through a copse of trees, and her thick eyebrows rocketed up. Her face was red. Sydney realized they were at the outskirts of the forest. Past Natalia was an open, grassy field.

Natalia yelled, and Sydney yelled, and they hugged. Sydney clutched Natalia as tight as she could. She never wanted to let go.

But Natalia gently pried Sydney away. "Girl," she said. "You stink."

She was grounded for a week. No texts, just email—so dorky. No socials either. She'd be twitching by the end of the first day.

But as the afternoon went on, it wasn't as bad as she'd thought it would be. Sydney sat on the back porch facing the wooded land that bordered her mother's property. With the sun dipping low, the temperature was bearable. After a long nap, she was pleasantly rested, the terror of the night before packed away. Easy to do now that she was safe.

The sliding door squeaked open, and her mother stepped outside, pink drink in hand. Sydney was not inclined to comment on the amount of alcohol her mother consumed per week. But it was enough to eclipse the modest amount Sydney had at parties. She couldn't help feeling a little self-righteous about that.

Despite her foibles, though, Sydney's mom was generally empathetic. Especially now that she might have lost her daughter.

"How you feeling, honey?" She bent over Sydney, smoothed her hair away from her face, and kissed her forehead. Sydney's mom didn't smell totally drunk yet—she was just getting started.

Sydney shrugged. "Fine, I guess."

"You don't want to talk about it?" Her mother sipped from the top of her glass, making that slurping sound Sydney found intolerable.

"Nothing to talk about."

Her mother sat back, worry lines creasing her forehead. A sign she needed her next Botox treatment. Sydney's mom was as beautiful as her daughter, but she'd begun losing herself in her quest to keep her looks. Trying to catch and keep them as if they wouldn't fade at all.

"It seems like a lot. Overnight in the woods?"

"I slept most of it."

Her mom's face was still twisted with concern. "You weren't scared?"

Sydney shook her head. She raised her knees to her chest and locked her fingers around them. "At first, maybe."

Her mom took another slurp, then sat back, her metal chair creaking as she did. Her expression evened out, now more pensive than anything. "That's a blessing, I guess."

Sydney didn't feel like responding. She only stared out at the mellowing sunset.

When her mother finally went inside, Sydney remained on the porch. The nap must have energized her. She felt like running, like pelting back into the woods. She couldn't squash the feeling rolling up inside her—that urge to leave this life behind, even the life contained in her phone. There was nothing left in her body except her heartbeat and the echo inside her own mind.

Eventually, though, she talked herself into staying put. Last night had been a weird experience, so of course she felt weird about it. Tomorrow was the first day of volleyball, and she had to be sharp. It was a given she'd make varsity, but she wanted to earn that place.

Sydney stood, stretched her legs. She padded back toward the screen door and nearly bumped her head against the ceiling.

Sydney hoisted her duffel against her hip as she stepped out of her Pilot. She already felt weak, like the sun had drained her. Remnants of Saturday still. She hoped her teammates would go easy on her. It would take a couple days, but she'd get back to her usual form.

Sydney headed toward the high school. Natalia waited on the sidewalk by the gym. "You okay?"

"Yeah, of course." Sydney tried to summon a smile. "Might take a few days to get back into things."

"You're not the only one. Even if you're the only one who got stranded overnight. People are out of practice."

Natalia shoved open the doors to the back half of the building. They went to a small rural school, so there wasn't much to it—just the gym, the locker rooms attached to the back, and a couple booths in the hallway used for games and the spring musical. Selling tickets, snacks, that kind of thing. Sydney's stomach growled at the thought. She hadn't eaten much the last few days, and she was suddenly starving. No wonder she was tired.

They shuffled into the locker room, where some of the other girls were already getting ready. "We need to get a burger after this," Sydney said.

"For sure. I'm doing intermittent fasting. My window ends around noon." Natalia dropped her bag and started rooting through it. "Just in time for the end of practice."

"You wanna drive out to Curtis?" The closest town with actual restaurants, movie theaters, Starbucks. Sydney was practically salivating at the thought of real meat. Maybe a steak.

Natalia pulled her top over her head and replaced it with her spandex shirt. "Yeah. Sure, I've got nothing else to do. A little low on cash though."

"I'll pay."

Natalia winked as she shimmied into her shorts. "I figured you'd be good for it."

Sydney sighed. She felt like she was moving through molasses. Everyone else was almost dressed, and she had to catch up.

She kicked off her jeans and stopped short.

Natalia did too. Sydney cringed as the frown crossed her friend's face. "What is wrong with your legs?"

The few girls left in the locker room turned to look. Sydney felt their eyes on her too, the weight of their judgment on her back. Her throat was thick. "I have no idea," she said, staring down at the mat of blonde hair coating her shins and thighs.

SYDNEY HASTILY REACHED for a pair of yoga pants she kept in case the gym was cold after practice. Her heart hammered.

They walked out onto the court, shoes squeaking on the freshly waxed floor. Natalia's jaw was tight. "What the hell, Sydney? Did you take, like, testosterone or something?"

"I have no idea." Tears pricked her eyes, and her stomach was in knots. Her entire body felt weird, like it wasn't her own. Those puberty videos from middle school had never warned them about something like this happening.

"Maybe you should see a doctor." Natalia's expression softened, and Sydney felt something in her body let go. "I'm so sorry. Whatever it is, maybe they can fix it."

Coach Cranston blew her whistle. "Let's go, ladies!"

Sydney ran toward the blue line that surrounded the court. She set her sneakers on it, willing the sudden hirsuteness from her mind. She wanted that empty feeling back, a feeling that would erase her embarrassment and hunger.

She wasn't tired anymore. The girls ran in a cluster, the heat from their bodies near. But she broke away from the pack, and then she was the only one in the gym. Her breath was even, her muscles stretching and moving, as she fell into an even rhythm. The stale school air whizzed by, kissing her cheeks.

Then there was a whistle again. But it was distant. She might have imagined it. Sydney kept running. She felt like she could run forever.

"Ms. Ross!" yelled the coach. "It's time for drills!"

Sydney came to a stop. She didn't even feel winded. She was more dazed, her blissful movement ended too soon.

Once they were finished with drills and sprints, they moved into formation for a practice game. It was oddly quiet apart from the slap of the volleyball and the squeaks of sneakers. Sydney felt hot under her pants. She felt the choke of the hair on her legs as it pressed against the tight fabric.

She started in the front row closest to the net. Lani Henderson was the server. She was small and quick, but sometimes her serves didn't have enough power. As the ball sailed toward the net, it looked like it wouldn't clear.

Sydney stepped into action. She bumped it, then slammed it down on the other side in a wicked spike.

The ball hit so hard that it deflated. The whine of its air was the only sound in the gym besides the hum of the A/C.

SHE LEFT PRACTICE EARLY, didn't bother to change. She had to stop herself from breaking the Pilot's hatch as she threw her duffel in.

On the way home, she couldn't think. She had to focus hard on the road, her vision splintering every time she turned her head. Her hands felt meaty, as if they'd grown three sizes, and she fumbled with the wheel.

Her mother's car was in the open garage. Sydney pulled up behind it, threw open her door, and lay down on the grass. The sun beat down on her back as she curled up like a turtle. Her tears soaked the spiky blades beneath her.

When she'd pulled herself together, she sat up. Carefully, Sydney closed the driver's side door. She could leave the duffel in the car.

First things first. *Find a mirror.*

There was noise in the kitchen, and then her mother emerged from the kitchen into the hallway. Before Sydney could even get to the bathroom.

"Oh!" Her mother clutched a goblet of wine. She already smelled of booze. "I didn't think you'd be home for a while."

"Neither did I." Sydney recoiled at her own voice. It was deep and froggy.

"What's wrong, baby?" Her mother came up to her, the wine sloshing in her glass, and laid a hand on her shoulder. "You seem upset."

Her mother had to be so drunk she couldn't even see straight. Either that or she was so grateful to see Sydney that she ignored her appearance. Little bit of both.

"Have to go to the bathroom," Sydney mumbled. Instead of heading to the downstairs bathroom as she'd originally intended, she banged her way up the stairs and flung herself into her room. Her breath was coming fast. It was in the top of her chest, unable to reach her belly.

The first thing she noticed was her hair. It was long and flowing, its usual burnished blonde, but now it encroached on her arms and neck. Her face remained pink, her lips in the familiar cupid's bow, and her eyes were still their usual blue.

She'd gained at least a foot on her old height, and her hands had indeed grown many sizes. Her feet threatened to bust out of her shoes, and she kicked them off before any damage could be done. The hair spilled out of her pants. Sydney stripped off her clothes and shrieked. It was everywhere now.

She ran her palms down her chest, her hips, her legs. It was soft, not like the coarse hair on a guy. At least she could console herself with the soothing texture under her hands. Maybe she could cut it and sell it for wigs.

"Sydney?" Her mother knocked on her door. "Do you want to talk about it?"

"No," Sydney called back. She climbed into her bed, pulled her covers over her. She could do nothing except fall asleep. Maybe when she woke up, all this would be gone.

IT MUST HAVE BEEN late afternoon when she woke up. The sun was still out, but muted. Sydney blinked, forgetting where she was, until she felt the hair on her skin. It was still there.

Her mother must have given up. She was probably face down on the couch, snoring away.

She couldn't show her face at practice, let alone school. She'd always wanted to be seen for her intelligence, for people to take her seriously, but this was the opposite of her natural beauty. Sydney was a monstrosity. And all because she'd been making out with Joey Carmichael in the woods, who wasn't even a good kisser.

*The woods.*

Sydney sat straight up. Her head was much closer to the ceiling than she remembered.

She wanted to hide. What better place to go?

Her mother was indeed snoring the snore of the wasted. Sydney snuck into the kitchen and grabbed a handful of lunchmeat from the fridge. As she swallowed it, she moved through the back porch doors. The air smelled of oncoming rain, clouds moving across the sky. Sydney jumped off in a flying leap and dashed into the forest.

This wasn't the woods where she and Joey had gotten lost. But somehow, Sydney had an innate sense of the terrain. She headed north. Her naked feet clung to the ground, keeping her from falling. She almost didn't realize she was unclothed. Her body blended in here.

Rain began sprinkling as Sydney rounded outside the development and crossed the street into another patch of trees. She had to get to the county park, where the party had been. They'd loitered in the pavilion past the sunset, ready to dash if anyone spotted a ranger. Her mind was sharper now, and she remembered it like a photo image. Him pulling her back through the trees, his hands around her waist, her falling into his side, her mind buzzing with the vodka Joey had filched from his parent's liquor cabinet.

She dropped to the ground, her knees hitting the gnarled roots of a big tree. Sydney howled, the mournful sound a cross between a human's and a wolf's.

There was that smell again. As crisp and sharp as the memory of that night.

That creature had come for her. She'd blocked it out. But it had, like, bitten her or something. Made her this way.

Sydney had never thought Sasquatches bred like vampires, but she'd also never thought either one was real.

The thought of such a creature putting its lips on her made her want to throw up. Instead, she got up, found her footing. She howled again, with more power this time, letting her anger pour through her body.

SHE KNEW the place when she found it. There was a rudimentary campsite, a burned-out fire. A shack of a building she hadn't noticed the first time. More of a hollowed husk, she realized when she peered into the hole that had once been a window. A protection from rain more than anything.

Sydney still smelled him, but it wasn't the same. The odor was more like a musk now. The same stink that clung to her. Regardless, it would take her to him, and that was the most important thing now.

The rain was coming faster. Sydney's hair stuck to her body, made her feel slow. She ducked into the shack and took stock of it.

His scent stuck to everything. Even if he wasn't here now, this was his territory. If she stayed here, he'd come back, especially if he wanted to get out of the rain. When she and Joey had gotten lost, it would have been easier if they hadn't separated. It made the most sense for her to stay put. Sydney tucked herself into a corner and waited.

She wasn't sure how long it had been when the grunts began coming from the door. He lumbered in, bowing his head, and slid to the floor just as she had. Standing in this room would not be comfortable for either of them.

"Well, hello," she said. "Remember me?"

He startled. So he did understand her.

"Wondering why I'm back?" Her voice had taken on a rumbling quality, coming out of her throat like thunder. It felt almost powerful. "I knew you would be."

He sounded like her but different. He seemed sad. The deep voice broke as he spoke.

"What did you do to me?" The rain pounded on the roof, making her sound dramatic. She kind of liked it. "Is this what gets you off? Turning teenage girls into Bigfoot? How do you even do it? It's fucking creepy is what it is."

The other one sighed. "You don't remember."

"Of course I don't fucking remember. I was knocked out. Or you don't remember either? Did you, like, drink my blood? Super gross, taking your MO from Dracula."

Sydney had never spit her thoughts out like this before. She felt something snap inside her as she talked. An anger that she'd held back pouring out of her like the rain.

He sighed again. "Okay, Syd. You can stop now. I've had enough."

Sydney blinked.

～

ONCE THE RAIN HAD ABATED, it was past nine. The woods were dark.

Sydney's dad fussed with a fire outside the shack. "Hard to do wet," he rumbled. "I'm guessing you're not going to want raw rabbit, though."

She crossed her arms. "I don't know how you're going to explain all this."

He looked up, his back still rounded from bending over the logs. "What's there to explain?"

"First I thought this was a vampire thing, but it's like... more of a werewolf thing?"

Her dad's shoulders sagged. He sat up, looked right at her. It was hard to see in the dark, but she could see the glinting of his big pupils. "You could say that."

"I'm just glad you didn't like, suck my blood. Ew." Sydney stuck out her tongue. "So am I gonna have to hide from school once a month?"

"It's a little more than once a month."

Now he pulled a lighter from... somewhere? Did Bigfoots have pockets? She watched the tiny flame spark against the wood, but nothing caught.

"Can you please stop being cryptic?"

Her memories of him were fractured, but she did remember him. He'd clutch her close and throw her in the air, or he'd spin her around until she was dizzy. He wasn't around a lot, but she knew he loved her.

"The thing is, honey..." He looked at her again, and this time she felt pierced, like he was running a needle right through her. "It's once a month that we're not... this way."

Sydney dropped her hands and stared. "What?"

"I hoped it wouldn't be like that for you. Since you're half human. And when you never grew the excess hair or got big, well... I really thought it would be different."

"But..." Her mind fought to process.

"My guess is the puberty hormones." Her dad tried the lighter one more time, but it only flickered and petered out. "You and that kid seemed pretty serious."

"Dad!" Sydney's face flamed. "You were watching?"

"Not exactly. I just wanted to make sure he wouldn't hurt you."

"Why didn't you say anything when you were chasing me?"

He gulped. "Honey, I've always tried to keep you safe. If I'd said something, you would have gotten scared. I wanted to make sure you got back okay. I think you saw me and passed out. So I stayed with you until morning and then left."

She stepped backward, carefully. Her bulk could easily snap the wet boards of the shack. She lowered herself to the ground and kept her gaze on him. "I still don't get how you put this past Mom for so many years."

He got up and moved toward his side of the cabin. Then a light flashed, and he smirked. She nearly gasped at the full sight of his face, surrounded by its hoary hair and oversized ears. "She knows."

The slimy ground stuck to Sydney's bottom, and she winced. "Something else you need to explain, Dad."

"There's that one time a month where we can walk free. She thought I was a lost hiker. But it only lasts for so long, and I woke up a giant in her bed." He swallowed. "When you were little, I used to come see you. But it got too much for her."

Sydney narrowed her eyes. "You have a phone?"

Her dad extinguished the flashlight and took another crack at the fire. This time the flames caught.

SYDNEY SLEPT FITFULLY. It didn't seem right to leave her dad. But she struggled to get comfortable on the hard ground, and he snored mightily all night. She woke before dawn.

He was still sleeping. She crept toward him, fully looking at his face. Despite the perpetual snarl from the constant snoring, she could tell he was resting comfortably from the way his limbs were limp.

She didn't want to bother him, but she had no way to leave him a note. His phone was dead, so she couldn't text him—and she wondered how he got power anyway. Did he sneak into libraries overnight? Use

Tesla charging stations? Finally, she picked up a leaf and a stick and scratched in the dirt as best as she could. *Be back.*

She picked her way back toward their place and finally staggered into the yard. The patio looked like an oasis.

Sydney hoped her mom had hauled her ass to work. But no... her mom stood in the kitchen, sucking down coffee from a chipped mug. As soon as she saw Sydney, she set it down and raced for her.

"Where have you been? I was so worried." Her mom picked up Sydney's phone and wiggled it in the air. "Why didn't you take it with you?"

Sydney's eyes were filling. She wondered what her mother thought at that moment. Sydney's hair dripped with mud. She was leaving stains. She wasn't wearing clothes. She had changed.

Her mom reached forward and threw her arms around Sydney. "Don't do that to me again."

"I need a shower," Sydney mumbled into her mom's nightgown.

"I know," her mom said.

Showering was different. The hair weighed her body down, making her dizzy. It frizzed up into little curls all over her. Swaths peeled off her and clogged the drain. At least washing the hair on her head was normal. Her long beautiful hair was intact, despite the awkward way it hung above her fur.

She dried off as best as she could. The sun was out, so it made the most sense to lie on her towel in the grass. The fence was high enough —the neighbors wouldn't see.

Sydney closed her eyes and let herself drift. Her mind felt so open these days. Like thoughts couldn't fully form. She wondered how her father managed to keep them afloat. Maybe he was accustomed to his life, his condition. Where had he come from? Were his parents still alive, hulking and hiding somewhere? Her Bigfoot grandparents.

When she sat back up—still damp—her mother was picking her

way through the grass. She held her own beach towel and a tall glass of whatever the pink drink was.

"Hold this?" She thrust the glass at Sydney. Sydney wrapped her big hand around it, careful not to crush anything.

Sydney's insides fizzed. It smelled strong, like vodka, and the scent clung to her mother's clothes. At least she wasn't in the robe anymore. She'd put on yoga pants and an athletic shirt. Suburban rich mommy clothes. But Sydney's mom had always worked. She'd never been one of those yummy mummies, not like the parents Sydney's friends had.

"Did you take the day off?" Sydney said delicately. Her voice felt wrong, too, with its new deep timbre. At least she could hear her own tones within, reassuring her she hadn't changed completely.

Her mother sighed as she draped the towel across the ground. "You could say that."

Sydney bit her lip and then spit it out as her facial hair brushed her mouth. "Did you lose your job?"

It had happened before, but Sydney had never gathered the courage to say anything. The last time, she'd been thirteen, too timid to bring up how scary the drinking was. How afraid she was that one day her mother would never wake up from passing out.

"I'm on suspension. They think I brought White Claw to work."

Sydney almost laughed but then remembered where she was and who she was listening to.

Her mother sat down and twined her legs around each other. Her legs were tan and smooth. She was still as beautiful as Sydney remembered, as if she'd never aged.

"Did you?" Sydney asked.

Her mother didn't answer. She picked a piece of grass and wrapped it around her finger.

Sydney was still holding the pink glass. A low growl sounded from inside her throat. She hurled the glass across the yard. It hit the deck and shattered into shards.

Her mother's eyes widened, her lips opening and closing like a fish's. But she didn't respond. She sat there and stared at Sydney. "You're different," she said.

"Duh," Sydney said.

"No. It's not that." It looked like tears glinted in her mother's eyes, but Sydney couldn't be sure. It was a warm day and neither of them were wearing sunglasses. "You've never said anything."

"I'm sixteen."

"I was waiting for the day this would happen." Now her mother buried her face in her hands, and Sydney knew she was crying. "Your dad said it might not. But here you are."

Sydney frowned. Something her dad had said tickled the back of her brain, but she couldn't remember. "Dad doesn't know about your drinking. I don't think."

"I know you were with him. I can smell it on you."

She couldn't follow the conversation. Sydney pinched the bridge of her nose. She wanted a sun umbrella now that most of her pelt was dry. "Okay, Mom," she started. "We're talking about two different things."

"Kind of," her mother admitted, raising her head. "Like I said, you've changed."

Sydney remembered. "Dad said you didn't care he was… what we are. That was why he wanted to be with you."

"I never said I didn't care." Her mom wrapped her arms around her own shoulders, hugging herself. "Does he think that?"

Sydney didn't reply.

"We clicked," her mom continued. "I liked talking to him. I found him fascinating. Different. And when his hair started to grow back, well… I knew there was a man hiding beneath all of… that."

She gestured at Sydney.

A hot flame of shame drove up through her. "So you still had a problem with the way he looked. With the way I look."

"No, no, it's not that." Her mother shook her head, her blond hair bouncing. "I mean, I can hardly see your faces. Who you are inside."

"Let's pivot," Sydney snapped. "Your drinking."

Sydney's voice was throatier now, louder, and her mother responded with a hissing "shhhhh," but she kept going.

"You need to get help," she said bluntly. "Do you not realize this is not good? It's like the most common stupid dependence out there. Not counting cigarettes and eating disorders."

"That's a horrible thing to say."

Her mother's face went blank. Sydney shifted uncomfortably on her towel.

They stayed silent for a few minutes. Sydney closed her eyes and listened to the bugs in the trees. The sun would be going down soon, leaving only the humidity and suffocating heat.

"I'll make you a deal," her mother said finally. "You go to volleyball tomorrow, and I'll find an AA meeting."

Sydney stared. "You can't be serious."

"If you keep missing practices, you won't be in the right shape."

Sydney scoffed. "Are you actually kidding me? Last time I destroyed one of the balls."

"Hard to do anything right the first time." Her mother glanced over at the wreckage of the glass near the deck. "Trust me."

SHE ROSE with the sun the following morning, wondering what Bigfoots did during the day. They were always lurking in the woods, right? Wouldn't they sleep more? Perhaps they lurked more during the day, and that was why they scared so many hikers.

She'd hoped to find herself transformed. Hoped to find herself back to Sydney Ross, the popular girl with the impossible body, the person people were drawn to like moths to a flame. But that hair still covered her, dragged her down.

Sydney found her mother sitting at the dining room table with her laptop. She was drinking a cup of coffee and scrolling through a list of AA locations. "Hi, honey," she said brightly. "I feel terrible, but I'm looking for help!"

That was good... right? Sydney licked her lips, spit out hair, and ambled into the kitchen for cereal and some of her own coffee.

"I also feel terrible," she said as she sat down with her mug.

"Second thoughts?"

"First thoughts." Sydney's fists clenched below the table. She watched the steam rise in a column from the hot liquid, not touching it yet. She was afraid she might burn it. "I never wanted to go to volleyball in the first place."

"I never wanted to stop drinking. Such a stupid habit," her mother said, sounding like acid. "But here we go."

*Also a stupid bargain.* "Fine," she said, lifting her hands out from underneath and holding the cup as lightly as she could. "Let's do it."

She went upstairs and ran the hair dryer along her entire body, getting out as much dampness as she could. It would take days to dry her pelt, but if she was going to volleyball, she couldn't dawdle. She brushed out the hair so it laid flat, then hesitated as she considered her beauty products. Finally, she put a flattening oil along her entire body, hoping to make the fur shine.

"Maybe I should be homeschooled," she said on her way out the door.

"No," said her mother.

SHE COULD BARELY FIT her bulk into the front seat, but she made it work. Sydney's meaty hands shook as she navigated the Pilot to school. She stayed in the car for as long as she could, watching the hairless teenagers laugh as they scampered up to the school. She spoke to whatever gods existed, asking for it all to shed. She'd vacuum the seats out as soon as practice was over.

She'd shoehorned her body into a pair of loose shorts and an oversized tee. Even though the hair covered all the private bits, she didn't want to risk anyone getting offended. Not that they would notice. Not after they realized what she was.

Sydney closed the driver's side door with a bang and sidled around to the hatch. She pulled it up and grabbed her bag. No turning back now.

Natalia was the first person she saw. She and Amy Weldon were giggling on their way to the locker room. With her new set of sensitive ears, Sydney could hear the words they murmured. "Do you think Sydney is ever coming back?" Amy asked. "Have you talked to her?"

Natalia made a face. "Something's wrong with that girl. I'd honestly ghost her."

Sydney's blood heated. She crept along as quietly as she could.

"Haven't you guys been friends for a long time though?" Amy asked. "I can't believe you would drop her like that."

Natalia shrugged. "It doesn't mean anything."

Sydney was about to roar, about to slap Natalia across the gym. Natalia would fly across the room, hit the lockers, sink to the floor. Her neck would be broken. No more time to betray Sydney.

But she thought about her dad. Everything he'd worked for, everything he'd given her.

She ran her hands through her long, silky hair, and her chest puffed up.

She was powerful now.

Sydney sidestepped and moved so that she towered in front of both girls.

Both of them screamed. People rushed out of the locker room, and they all started screaming too.

Sydney smirked. Everyone knew who she was.

# THE PORTRAIT OF INDRID COLD

As he pads through the living room in his slippers, Bernie notices the moving truck across the street. He's been feeling much better since Brenda Lowell sold that house. The woman was insufferable. He had to turn up his game shows to drown out the incessant barking of those rat-dogs.

His neighborhood is for single people who have lost spouses. Fifty-five and up. Bernie's wife died three years ago—ovarian cancer—and he hadn't wanted to stay in their house a moment longer. As he packed up his things and removed hers, he'd hoped for a new start in Willow Ridge.

Bernie watches two men unload a dark-stained hutch into Brenda's ex-front door. Willow Ridge is a good place for a person to disappear. The houses are all the same, stout gray brick and beige siding and white trim. They are meant to look modern yet utilitarian. An ideal environment for the practical widower. Each boasts a small patch of yard that is mowed once a week by a mustachioed landscaper.

Bernie has never liked routine. Sometimes he wishes he'd picked a more chaotic place. An artist's hamlet, perhaps, or a mountain cabin. He'd get a dog and cook outside. He would not need a landscaper because there would be no yard to mow. Just dirt and trees and the sunrise if he was up early enough to catch it.

Andrea insisted on this development because they thought he would become old and infirm. Right now, he is seventy-five and totally fine. He walks through the neighborhood every day. At odd hours, of course, because he does not like to be predictable. Sometimes he wakes at two in the morning and checks which houses still have lights on.

The movers are in and out, in and out. Bernie decides to get a beer and sit outside on his small porch. The Corona is cold in his hand as he eases into his camping chair. He plunks it in the cupholder and slides a pair of aviators onto his face. Just in case anyone thinks he is spying.

He scratches the top of his head. Still got that rough, stubbly coating. Not his old hair, but at least he's got time left.

Bernie drinks a Corona or three before the truck is finished, sending diesel fumes in its wake. No sign of a new neighbor though.

He's about to go in when a different truck pulls into the driveway. It almost looks like an armored car. Bernie tries to remember when he's seen them in movies or outside banks. The sides and front are steel gray. The truck is boxy, no real shape to it.

Three different men hop out of the cab and push a sliding door along the side of the truck. Bernie can't see what they're retrieving. He squints and finally makes out a large, covered object balanced carefully between the movers.

It's flat, and they're having trouble getting a grip on it. "Shit," yells one, loud enough for Bernie to hear. He'd listened to Rebecca when she told him to get a hearing aid.

"He's gonna murder us if you break that thing," shouts another.

Meanwhile, the garage door is opening and another man is suddenly there. Bernie can't make out all his features, but he can tell the guy is pale, graying, and very tall. This must be his new neighbor.

"You do not need a dog."

This from Bernie's daughter, who stands in his kitchen with her hands on her hips. She looks so much like Becky: small, upturned nose and pale, freckled skin. Perpetually sunburned, fine brown hair pulled into a high ponytail.

Bernie, sitting at his kitchen table, thinks a dog is a good reason to walk around the neighborhood more often. Maybe a golden retriever. Something big and fluffy.

"I'm lonely," he says to his daughter.

Andrea rolls her eyes. "Then get out in the community. We wanted you to live here for a reason, right? Activities for the AARP set?"

Bernie does not want to play euchre at the neighborhood center.

"It would be fun," he says. "Learning how to take care of a dog. I'm not too old to learn something new."

"Are you too old to vacuum hair from all over the place?" Andrea sighs and sits down across from him. "You don't need to be any messier in here."

"It's not messy." He scowls, feeling the deep cuts around his mouth. Bernie takes care of himself. He's not infirm. He doesn't need anyone to take care of him. He took care of Becky, after all, and he did a damn good job. Every day hurt: putting in the work to help her while slowly crumbling himself. So what if the house is a little cluttered.

She scoffs. "Look at it. You might as well be a hoarder."

He bristles. "Hey. Just because you're forty doesn't mean you get to boss me around."

But Andrea had bossed him around, in a way. After Becky died, Bernie let his girl run the show while he was empty with grief. He can't assume his daughter will know that he wants to take back control.

"It won't be healthy to bring an animal in here with stuff all over the place." Andrea gestures vaguely at his piles of newspapers and thrift-store record albums. "I think you should let it go, Dad. I'll get you a zoo pass."

Around midnight, Bernie slips out his front door and ambles onto the sidewalk. He keeps that leisurely pace as he passes beneath the community's carefully selected streetlights. They are ornate, lamps really, like the kind you'd find in a historical movie. They make the night less stark.

He takes the long way around the neighborhood, passing the community center and the pool. There's a main road adjacent to the complex. Traffic zips past him, still loud and steady at the late hour.

Once he's pointed back toward his street, he observes the homes. All the same. What distinguishes them is what's going on inside. The few illuminated windows show big-screen TVs blasting or people curled up with books. Not many salacious actions going on here. If there were, they'd be in the bedrooms, because no one wants that kind of gossip spread about them. Bernie chuckles to himself. Maybe eighty-year-old Muriel Parker is a pot dealer. Kinda makes sense, with all the joint pain going on around here.

Bernie turns right and crosses to the other side of his road.

The new neighbor's house is right there. And Bernie's already on that side. No harm in passing by.

It's eerily quiet without Brenda's bastard dogs. Bernie enjoys it. He'll take a brief pause and return to his business. He's getting tired, anyway. It's nearly time for Biofreeze and Game Show Network before he falls asleep.

There is only one light on, near the back of the house. It's glowing a light green. Interesting color choice–maybe the neighbor wants to show that he's different. Or maybe his new neighbor is the drug dealer. Muriel's too old for the operation.

Before he can think differently, Bernie is creeping up to the window, cutting between two yards. He has to be quiet, since Jan Leavensworth will tell everyone if she sees him sneaking through here. Jan's lights are out, so he hopes she's asleep.

His knees cry for mercy as he crouches down. Then, carefully, he raises himself to the window's height.

The room inside is dark, made more so by the deep brown wood accenting the walls. It doesn't look like a Willow Ridge house, more like a mini-mansion. He doesn't remember Brenda's place having this kind of decor. Bernie can barely see anything beyond the main focus of the room.

A painting stares back at him. A portrait from old-timey days. A lush red background behind the subject, surrounded by an intricate golden frame.

And that subject: a man who seems to stare right into Bernie's eyes.

And he smiles. And smiles. And smiles.

BERNIE COULDN'T SLEEP last night. He never wants to be anywhere near that room again. He feels strange even being across the street from it, like it's invaded his space. *I was here first*, he thinks as he sits on his back porch drinking coffee. It's the furthest place he can be from that painting.

It is a nice day, the sun warm on his face. He'll be able to sit here until eleven-ish, when the day will get too hot. After that, he doesn't know what he will do. The coffee scorches Bernie's tongue, but he shivers. He needs to get out for the day.

Bernie decides to visit the public library. He doesn't have Internet at home—just email and apps on his cell phone. Usually, he doesn't need more than that, but this situation calls for a different approach.

He pulls into the parking lot and gets out slowly, his knees aching. Sometimes he feels like a young man in a wretched body. He shouldn't be like this, shouldn't feel this way. His body breaking down day by day.

The computer area is nice, privacy screens creating a little bubble around him, comfortable chairs. He knows the librarians like him because he knows how to log in and print by himself.

"Hey, Bernie." Clarissa is helping another patron at the computer across from him. Bernie nods at her. He Googles "painting of weird smiling man."

The images come up, and Bernie grimaces. The first thing he sees is the painting he recognizes. He closes the window right away.

Is it a portrait of the man who lives there?

Bernie used to be attractive, with his aquiline nose and blue eyes and strong jaw. Now he has jowls and lines. Liver spots. He's shrinking. Andrea should use an older picture for his obituary, like she did for Rebecca. But he'd never age like this man: the smile that won't end, the stare of the black-ringed eyes.

He blinks. He'll have to open the article again. He needs to know what this is.

Once he pulls it back up, he winces and scrolls so he doesn't have to see the painting. He reads about a man called Indrid Cold, born from a West Virginia legend. Sighted by another man, Woodrow Derenberger, in 1966, the smiling man found his way into rural folklore. A man who spoke telepathically, who was completely normal except for that smile.

Bernie rubs his hands along his upper arms. His fingers feel like icicles.

"You okay?" Clarissa has finished with the other patron. She looks concerned. One lock of neon pink hair falls over her eye.

He nods. "Everything's fine, yeah."

"You look cold. Is the AC too high? I can check with the building manager."

Bernie shakes his head. "I'll be fine. I'll only be here a few more minutes anyway."

Clarissa smiles. "Okay then! Let me know if you need anything."

It's strange, but even Clarissa's smile disturbs him.

He blinks. Maybe he does need help. "You know what?" he asks her. "Do you know how to look up property records?"

She brightens. "Of course! I'll show you how to get on the county site."

Clarissa drags up a chair and gently pushes the privacy screen over, careful not to get too close to the other patrons. Soon they're bending over the monitor, scrutinizing the entries on the tax site. The tiny words swim as he squints at them. "You're gonna have to help me read it," he says.

She points to Bernie's name. "Here's where it shows you own your house. What address are you looking for? I love a good mystery."

He pauses. He doesn't want to tell Clarissa. It's hard to say no to her shining face, but his skin is crawling. Bernie knows Clarissa is a normal person. He's seen her at the reference desk a hundred times. Even if he never talks to her, he says hello and she says hello back. He doesn't know about her personal life, but that's okay. He doesn't need to.

If this man is loose in the community... could he turn everyone into smiling men? Was that something they did? Would Clarissa become a smiling woman, her hands tucked up into her armpits, manic with her pink hair swirling in the wind?

He points to the screen. "Across the street from mine."

THEIR SLEUTHING REVEALS that the owner of the home is one Irving Coleman, age sixty-seven. A former art archivist. He'd lived in New York most of his life but has returned to Ohio to be with family. At least according to the press articles they found.

Clarissa hums. "He doesn't sound too menacing. Kinda famous, actually! Hope that helps you sleep at night!"

Bernie doesn't want to be weird. This isn't a novel where a crotchety old man bonds with a sweet librarian over their shared love of books. Things here are professional.

"Sure. Thank you," Bernie says, getting up from the computer as Clarissa returns to the desk.

He doesn't know who to discuss this with. His daughters will call him insane. Rebecca would have understood, but she's not here. It's taken him long enough to accept that. He can't go back and pretend he can talk to her. She's not a ghost.

Bernie drives home and hoists himself up out of the car. It's balmy and sunny: perfect weather. He grits his teeth and looks over at Irving Coleman's house. It can't be a coincidence that he has the same initials as Indrid Cold.

The house is shut up tight. No car in the driveway, no lights on–

although it is the middle of the afternoon. Could Irving Coleman be working? Some people in the neighborhood still work. Retirement dates are creeping up and up these days.

Even if Coleman isn't there, it wouldn't be a good idea to check out the house again. Even in broad daylight.

But maybe the picture wouldn't be so scary then.

BERNIE EASES himself through the front door and reaches into the fridge. He pops the top of his beer and takes a deep drink. It's the chill of the liquid more than anything that invigorates him. He isn't slaking thirst or enjoying the overly hoppy flavor. He doesn't even need the alcohol, only the cold on his tongue.

He walks to the front bay window and pushes the curtains to the side. Clocks the location of the painting and gets a shiver. His gaze slides down the street, moving across the homes he's spied on many times. The woman who walks around in her underwear. The couple who are always watching the latest HBO drama. The man whose house is a hoarded mess behind sloppy blinds—and Andrea says *Bernie's* bad.

Who lives next door to Irving Coleman? They must have been just as happy as Bernie was to see Brenda Lowell go. But there's a hole in his mind when it comes to that neighbor. He doesn't remember ever meeting or seeing them.

He's about to consider going over there when he hears a knock. Then the doorbell.

"Hang on, hang on, I'm coming," he growls. It's probably Andrea. She likes to check on him at the most inopportune times, even leaves work on her lunch break to visit.

Bernie whips the door open and finds himself face-to-face with Brenda Lowell.

Tears streak her heavy eyeshadow and mascara, and her normally thin lips sag in a pout. She's sobbing, rubbing her eyes, only making her look more like a clown.

Bernie frowns.

"I know what you're gonna say." Brenda hiccups. "I'm back because I have a problem."

He braces himself on the door frame with a palm. "I'm sorry."

"Peanut wasn't with me when my kids came to move me out." She wrings her hands. "There was a miscommunication. I thought Katie had her, and Katie thought I had her."

Bernie furrows his brow. "How far away did you move?"

"Solon. Katie wanted me to be closer for the kids." She swats at her cheeks.

"Why'd you come back? You could've called me."

She goggles. "I barely know you."

"Then why are you here now?"

Brenda stomps a pink-fringed cowboy boot. Bernie has never seen such hideous footwear.

"I had to come back and look for Peanut. But I can't find her anywhere."

"Do you want to come in?" Bernie's knees are getting tired, and Brenda looks wrecked. She elbows past him and perches on the armchair that is mainly there because the girls thought it would be a nice addition to the living room. "Want a beer?" he asks her.

Brenda sniffs. "Sure."

He shuffles into the kitchen and pulls out a Corona, then snaps the cap off and returns to the living room. Brenda doesn't complain about the brand. She takes the cold bottle. Their fingers touch for a second. He lets out a grunt as he falls into his chair, the one with the seat carved in for his butt.

Bernie isn't sure about conversation, so he keeps it to the dog. "Do you think she's in the house? Or did she get away?"

"She didn't leave the house except to take walks. I don't know what she would have done if she was outside on her own." Brenda looks at him. "You haven't seen anything strange going on around that house, have you?"

"Not really." He wouldn't have seen the painting if he hadn't snooped. "Guy is weird, though. I've only seen him outside the once. Ordering some kids around."

She nods. He imagines the catharsis of her tears. He's no stranger to that feeling. She'll feel better until they well up again.

Bernie hedges before he confesses. "But I did go poke around the other day."

Brenda is a funny woman. She dyes her hair pitch black and paints that makeup all over the full face. It doesn't cover the lines. She's as old as he is but can't accept it.

He watches her as she raises her eyebrows. "What did you see?"

"He's got some weird painting in his basement. Creeped me out." Bernie can't believe he's telling this to Brenda Lowell. Can't believe he's even talking to the woman. He's said more words to her than he did when she lived here. "It just stares and smiles. I couldn't have something like that in my house."

Brenda shivers. "I hope my baby isn't in there with that awful thing."

"Do you want to stay here for a little while?" Bernie nearly slaps his mouth, the words out unbidden.

She doesn't reply, just stares.

"We could look for Peanut together," he clarifies.

Brenda relaxes, almost smiles. "That would be nice."

Jan Leavenworth isn't home, so they start with the neighbors on the other side of Coleman's house. Brenda remembers them: the Spiellers. An unassuming couple, no one special. Forgettable.

Brenda side-eyes Coleman's house as they walk across the street. "I hope he's not looking."

"We're not doing anything wrong." They move slowly, since Bernie's knee aches. Brenda's feathered hair flaps in the wind. She steps up, rings the bell. Bernie stands behind her.

A young woman answers the door. For a second, Bernie's teenager mind flares. She's young and pretty, tan skin, green eyes. Hair a man could bury himself in, brown with blond highlights. But those green eyes are puffy and red.

"Hello?" Her voice is a squeak. "Can I help you?"

"We're looking for the Spiellers," Bernie says at the same time Brenda asks the girl if she is okay.

The woman looks between them both. Her lip trembles. "I'm Sara. Their daughter."

"Do you remember me?" Brenda points to the house next door. "I used to live there. Sorry about my dogs."

Sara's eyes flare. "That fucking house."

Brenda steps back, but Sara holds up a hand and continues. "I'm sorry. It's not you. It's that man. I don't… I can't even tell you."

Bernie has decided to stay quiet. He watches the interaction as his brain ticks.

"What happened?" Brenda asks.

They are standing at an awkward angle, Bernie and Brenda on the top stair, Sara behind the screen door. The Spiellers' daughter opens it then, inviting them inside.

The house is quiet, cold, the AC humming. Bernie and Brenda approach the dining room table, which is appended to the kitchen, same as in Bernie's house. The entire open floor plan is sparkling clean, as if no one had ever lived there.

"Can I get you some water? Tea?" Sara gestures awkwardly. They all know that Bernie and Brenda will not be asking for beverages. So Sara falls into the chair across from them, exhaling.

Brenda doesn't have to prompt her to speak this time. "My parents are missing," Sara says.

Bernie makes an effort to keep his face slack. Calm.

Brenda, being herself, can't do that. She explodes in pity. "Oh God, my dear, I'm so sorry." She reaches over to pat Sara's arm, and the girl flinches. Brenda doesn't seem to notice.

"It's just so bizarre." Sara wipes a tear. "I mean, not that I really want to talk about it. But since you're neighbors, maybe you would know something. About that house."

Bernie's body fills with pins and needles. He and Brenda exchange a look. He can't believe he's playing detective with her.

"Well," Brenda begins. "When I moved away, Peanut got lost. I'm afraid she's gone for good."

Bernie is surprised that his ex-neighbor can control her wailing and gnashing of teeth. Maybe he has a new respect for her.

He senses that now he must contribute. "I went over there. That Coleman is strange."

Sara's eyes widen. She speaks carefully. "How so?"

"He's got this strange picture in his basement." Bernie's got a frog in his throat. He coughs. It's like the words don't want to leave him. "It's of a man just smiling. It felt..."

Sara's body tenses. "Dangerous?"

Now they are a trio.

Brenda goes to OfficeMax and purchases a large whiteboard along with dry-erase markers. She tacks it to Bernie's dining room wall. He doesn't care. If his daughter pries him from the house, she'll have to plug and paint over the holes.

Sara has accepted water and a beer. She is slumped in the chair beside Bernie. Brenda stands in front of the whiteboard, assuming a righteous pose. It's like she's forgotten Peanut is gone.

"Okay, so this is what we have." Brenda writes *Spiellers* and *Peanut* at the top of the whiteboard. Below, she writes *Picture* and *Creepy Smiling Man.*

"It's not really a picture," Bernie offers. "More like a portrait."

Brenda claps her hands together. "A portrait. Go on."

Bernie doesn't really have anything to go on from. "Um, it had a gold frame. Looked old."

Sara sits up a little. "Like the portrait of Dorian Grey?"

The reference feels familiar, but Bernie can't place it. Until Brenda snaps her fingers. "Yes! That was the story where the guy wasn't aging because his portrait was."

"Oscar Wilde. We read it in my Fiction Analysis class. I'm majoring in English." The girl blinks, and the hair on her arms stands up with goosebumps. "But this isn't totally like that."

Bernie shakes his head. "The picture and the man are pretty much the same."

Brenda writes *Picture + Man = Vulnerable?*

"We still don't know…" Sara swallows. "Why they were even over there."

"There have been some strange noises," Bernie says.

Brenda sniffs. "They did not like my dogs."

"They don't like a lot of noise. Mom liked to make these junk journals. Like, she'd make the bindings and sew in pages that she could write on. She needed quiet."

Bernie thinks of the Spiellers' house, quiet as a tomb.

They are all hitting a wall. The sun is going down outside his back window. He asks Sara quietly if she wants another beer, and she shakes her head.

"Do you think they're dead? He killed them with his smile?" Brenda's hands are shaking.

"I saw the man, and I didn't die," Bernie says.

Sara's stare is on him, and her voice has an edge. "I wonder why."

"Maybe it's because he didn't look directly at me." Bernie covers his eyes as if Irving Coleman is standing right in front of them. "I only saw the portrait."

There is silence.

Sara grits her teeth, stands. "They're not dead. We're going to go find them."

THEY CAN'T DECIDE whether to go that night or during the day, since it's unclear when Coleman is at home. The dark might make it more difficult, Brenda reasons. Eventually, Sara falls asleep on Bernie's couch, and Brenda takes the guest room.

Bernie is alone in his bedroom. He can't sleep. His back hurts. He keeps staring out his window, watching the house, watching broken streetlamps flickering. Isn't that what they pay the HOA for?

It's so quiet. He's forgotten Brenda's dogs even existed.

He thinks of the librarian, the websites they looked at. Why would a man like Indrid Cold—Irving Coleman, whatever—choose a fifty-five-plus retirement community to settle down? Why take out his rage on unsuspecting septuagenarians and rat-dogs? Why rage at all?

Maybe he's an idiot, but he wanders out into the darkened living room. Sara's brows are crossed in her sleep, her lips turning down, her body pulled into the fetal position. A wave of shame hits him for noticing her attractiveness earlier. She reminds him of his girls. Andrea in particular. Andrea was so peaceful at rest, such a difference from her daytime personality.

Becky is there then, a ghost at his side, and pain lances through him. She's looking down at Andrea too. The air is cold at her arrival. He can't see her, but he knows she is there.

This house pulses with pain. Brenda's loss, Sara's loss. His loss.

Bernie sighs and pulls back the gossamer front curtains. That broken streetlamp flickers in front of Coleman's house.

HE CREEPS across the street on soft feet, Swiss Army knife tucked into his pants pocket, a crowbar in one hand.

He's never broken into a house before. Doesn't have the skill to pry open a window. But Coleman is a night creature. No matter what Bernie does, the smiling man will find him. So he just has to be quick. Smash the window, climb inside.

As long as Bernie saves Sara and Brenda, it won't matter if he dies. Andrea will sell his house, but she'd be free of him. Bernie doesn't know jack about the afterlife, yet any chance of Becky's presence could lure him there.

When he gets to the side of the house, he assesses the window. It's tall enough that he'll need to hoist himself off the ground, but not too tall that he'll have to climb. He can reach the bottom of the pane from here, but he can't kick the window open. "Time for my little friend," Bernie mutters.

He swings the crowbar. It hits the window with a satisfying crash. Glass tinkles down around him. He smashes the bottom pane a few more times, then grabs the sill. Winces as his back screams. Broken shards tear at his clothes.

There's a scuffle from inside, muddled voices. Coleman's minions.

Bernie struggles, his abdomen stretching against the windowsill. He's perched at an awkward angle, legs flailing. Searching for a center of gravity. He squirms forward, and his feet find the wood molding. Bernie falls onto a plush antique rug.

He's in.

Three big men rush into the room and fall on him. He is pummeled, fists flying against his face, beating bruises into his skin. He is no match for them, but an otherworldly strength lifts him. The crowbar is still in his hand. He swings it, and it tears through the air, knocking the men back. They smell like sweat and rage.

Behind them, Coleman stands, that smile plastered on his face.

When he meets Bernie's eyes, he doesn't blink. He extends one finger in a "come here" gesture.

The painting is right in front of him, that smile reflecting in it.

Bernie hesitates. Men are groaning on the floor behind him. The smiling man continues to smile. Now he has crossed his arms across his chest, waiting. He knows Bernie will give in. *They always do.*

It's as if Coleman is wrapped around his brain stem.

Bernie's breathing slows. He takes a step back. Far back enough that he can see the whole of the picture, even if he has to crane his neck a little.

"What's wrong?" Coleman's voice is as cold as he is. "Don't you want me to paint you?"

"You bastard." Bernie spits on the ground. A knot of saliva and throat residue falls from his lips. He gasps, coughs until it's all out, and resumes his speech. "You evil demented bastard."

Coleman doesn't move. His eyes glint red, a special beckoning just for Bernie.

No. Bernie will not yield.

He flips the knife out of his pocket and runs for the portrait.

The blade is dull. He must drag it through the canvas once, twice, three times to make an indent. Bernie's dreams of slashing triumphantly scatter. He is hacking now, like he's trying to cut through a piece of wood with a butterknife.

Coleman steps closer. "It won't work, Bernard. Why don't you give that up. Talk to me."

Bernie doesn't turn around, doesn't look at Coleman. He shakes the painting, wanting to angle it off the wall, as his back screams. Bernie twists the sides of the frame, pulling as hard as he can, and it flies off the wall. Now it's on the floor, and he has unfettered access. Now he can dig the knife as far as he wants. Makes holes in the canvas, stabs the weapon into Coleman's eyes.

When Bernie turns to see Coleman, the man is on his knees. Blood spills from his eyes. He puts his hands over his face, and the blood is like tears filtering through his fingers. He gasps for air.

The men on the floor are struggling to their feet. Bernie plans his escape, quickly, frantically. He can go out the front door now that he is inside.

The men are groaning. The men are crying.

"My boys," croaks Coleman. "I love you."

"I love you so much, Dad," says one of the men, reaching down to embrace Coleman. They are smiling through their tears.

And then Bernie sees them: shadows, turning a corner, red eyes peeking out of the dark.

BERNIE MOVES AS QUICKLY as he can on his old legs. He pounds up the stairs and dashes through the living room. He stops only to notice the many portraits hanging on the walls, the familiar faces with the freshest paint. Peanut. The Spiellers. There's not much time, but he has to stop. They're not as big as the others, so he grabs them and shoves them under his arm before running across the street.

"We have to go," Bernie says breathlessly as he plunges through his front door.

Sara sits up, bleary-eyed. "Huh?"

"Coleman. It's not safe." He blubbers. Yells for Brenda. She pads out into the hallway, yawning, her hair every which way.

"What's wrong?" she asks.

Bernie grabs her hand, feels an electric shock go through them, probably from Brenda's feet connecting with the carpet. "We gotta go."

He shoves the paintings into his trunk. They pile in, breathless, as Bernie peels out and squeals away into the night.

THEY ROLL into his daughter's driveway around two in the morning. He calls her cell, but there's no answer. Brenda is asleep in the passenger seat, Sara curled in the back.

He's woken by a hard tap on the window. Andrea's face hovers behind the glass. He shoos her away from the door and pops it open, groaning as he hoists himself out.

"What are you doing here, Dad? And who are all these people?"

Brenda is stirring. Bernie looks over to her with a kind of fondness. He sighs. "Long story."

Andrea calls off work and ushers the groggy trio into her living room. Bernie's daughter has a huge house, a custom build, the kind that screams wealth. They fall onto the dove-gray couches that surround an immense flat-screen TV. Sara is shaking, and Andrea hands her a blanket.

Now they are a quartet.

Bernie gives her the short version. He considers leaving out the unbelievable parts, but she needs to know everything if she's going to help them.

His daughter's eyebrows are high enough to kiss her hairline. She doesn't speak, just looks to the other two women. They nod.

"I don't believe it," Andrea keeps saying. She makes coffee and hands it out. Sara declines, but the rest of them are desperate for it. Bernie requests ibuprofen on the side.

"It's a tough one to swallow." Bernie swallows his own pill. He wishes the truth were that easy for Andrea to understand. It's hard to look at her. Becky reimagined.

Brenda rubs her eyes. Sunlight from the closest window illuminates her eye lines and dry lips. She seems so much older, like she's been through a war.

Bernie gets it. Indrid Cold has aged him too, and not like a good wine. He turns to Brenda. "Can I drop you off at your new house? We can find another way to get your car."

She blinks. "Is it too late?"

"For what?"

"Peanut."

Bernie has forgotten the paintings in the car. He gets up and hobbles outside, lifts them out from the trunk, brings them inside. The women gawk.

"What does it mean, though?" Andrea, all curious. "I mean, when you destroyed his portrait, the guy died. So what about these?"

Bernie takes another glug of coffee, as if the caffeine can help him process the possibility. It's bitter.

Sara and Brenda exchange looks, and Andrea stares pointedly back at her father.

"He asked if he could paint me," Bernie says, thinking hard. His brain isn't as quick as it used to be. "Maybe that would turn me into one of his minions." He'd seen those shadows—could they have been living?

Sara moves closer to the picture of her parents, which leans against Andrea's dining room table. They are pleasant, smiling, calm. "We need to be careful with these," she says. Her voice is haunted.

～

BACK TO WILLOW RIDGE, now with Andrea.

And alongside the portraits, two gallons of white paint in the trunk.

It's odd, being surrounded by them all. A nest of people, lives entwined with his, people he'd usually avoid. He knows the pierce of loss that follows them, yet they may have hope to get them back. Becky is gone for good.

Late afternoon now, the sun glowing as it heads to the east. He's crushed, his body afire, fatigue filling every cell of him.

"We'll go now," Sara says. She's perked up, her cheeks flush with color. "We never even saw those bad guys, Bernie."

"There are four of us now," Brenda adds. "They're no match."

Bernie would disagree, especially considering the size of those men.

But it's daytime, and Coleman's window is still broken, covered haphazardly by duct tape. It's easy enough to break through and for them all to hoist themselves through the window. The younger women pass the paint through, the gallons half-cracked open, followed by the portraits. They'd decided it would be better to do the deed at the house, in case it didn't work from a distance.

Bernie feels a sudden nausea. Like he isn't supposed to be here.

"I'm staying back." He slides down onto the blood-red carpet, back scraping against the wall under the window.

Andrea turns. "Dad. You have to come. You're the only one who knows where to go."

"I don't, though." Bernie's voice turns gravelly, his throat clogged with mucus. "You're not looking for Cold. Coleman. You're looking for your dog. And your parents."

The drawing room—for that's what this is, an old-man drawing room that does not belong in Willow Ridge—smells like rot. Dust. Blood.

Andrea wrinkles her nose. "Do you want me to stay with you?"

He shakes his head. "You don't need me. I'll be here."

Sara and Brenda frown. But Andrea is his girl, the one who always matched wits with Becky, headstrong and driven. She sets her chin, grabs a paint gallon, and marches forward.

❦

BERNIE DOZES. He isn't sure how long they've been gone. His neck has a crick from lining it up against the windowsill.

A clunk sounds from somewhere beside him. The house settling, a critter in the walls. Nothing major.

Then there's another clunk. A sweep of hard metal, like a chain being pulled along the floor.

He pops up out of sleep, groans as he stands up. The thumping is close by, but he can't tell where it's coming from.

Bernie is about to head into the house to see how the paint job is going when the things enter.

The women aren't there. No, it's a cluster of people, heading right for him. The grunting progeny of Indrid Cold lead the pack, incandescently smiling, like lamps left on too long. At their feet is a tiny chihuahua, jaws spread in an otherworldly echo of the men's. And behind the dog, the Spiellers. The wife, beautiful like Sara, saliva dripping from her lips. The husband, tall and stoic, the kind of man Bernie should have been, but now he smiles unhinged like the rest of them.

Not people anymore. Monsters.

Bernie trips on the edge of the carpet as he inches back toward the window. They are advancing, too close.

He braces himself. What will death feel like?

He's waited so long to be with her again. He's been a shell throughout these days, living, but not really. If he closes his eyes, if he yields to them, it will happen fast. Will consume him like the fire that took Becky.

The last time he saw her was in the funeral home, minutes before they rolled her body into the crematorium. The service was over; the mourners had their chance to say goodbye. Bernie wore a black suit with a blue shirt and tie. People asked him if blue was Becky's favorite color, and he lied. It was the only dress shirt he had.

He knew she was gone. He wasn't that dumb. She'd left after she breathed out that last time. But her body was part of their story. All the times they'd fumbled around in bed, moving quietly so the girls wouldn't hear them. When they'd pressed themselves close, their breath hot and mingling, and it was like the clock had stopped ticking.

When she rebuffed him because she was nursing or exhausted and he struggled not to take it personally, but he knew her body had grown and stretched and created those two little girls, had fed and nourished them, and he turned over to let her be with herself. And when the girls had gone, and when the cancer came, and the only place he could find her was next to him.

She was the other soul to his, the match.

And he said goodbye to her body.

The mob is nearly to him. He smells their breath, their sweat. He's ready to let go.

*Unless.*

Bernie roars. Pulls himself up and barrels through them. The dog pounces, grabs his pant leg with its teeth, and Bernie shakes it off.

He remembers Cold the first day he moved in, wondering if the man would be friendly. Remembers watching the boys as they helped him. Like they were a normal family, Cold a man who'd lost his wife, new to that neighborhood of loss. Willow Ridge and its willows, bending toward water, mourning.

Cold must have had a wife, Bernie thinks, taking the stairs that cut the parlor in half, screaming for Andrea and Sara and Brenda. Where else would those boys have come from?

He's at a dead end. Backed into a corner at the end of a hallway. They're coming for him.

He falls through a door and into a dark, opulent room. There's a four-poster bed, another one of those plush carpets—purple this time —and the cloying scent of strong perfume. The kind a woman would wear. There's no room to stumble around, no room to breathe. He can't hide. He's done.

Then the dog snaps to attention. It's closest to him, on the floor, eyeing him up.

The strange smile falls off its face. It runs up into his lap and slurps his cheeks, blocking his vision, radiating its musty dog smell into his nose. There's confused chatter from the Spiellers too, and the wife screams when she realizes she's being crowded by frantic smiling lugs of men. Boys. Men.

He smells the paint, heavy and heady. Sara and Brenda and Andrea are throwing it onto all the pictures they can find.

Bernie backs up, but there's nowhere else to go, and he hits the wall. He jostles against the end table beside the bed. Framed photos rain down on him. The dog is snarling and the smiling men are coming and the Spiellers are screaming. Too much, too much.

One photo falls in his lap. It's a real photograph, not a painted portrait. A family.

Cold—Coleman—stands over his three sons. They're babies, the oldest not more than ten. The man's ever-present smile looks softer somehow, proud. A woman clings to Coleman, her arms on two of the boys' shoulders. Her lips are tipped up and she looks happier than anyone has ever been.

Bernie doesn't have time to decide. He rips the back off the frame, his fingers find the photo, and he pulls it out and rips it up.

All three men droop. The smiles wash from their faces. They stand, confused. Bernie's sure they're going to drop dead right then.

But Indrid Cold's—Irving Coleman's—boys start crying. Weeping. Sobbing. Falling into each others' arms.

Bernie is still shoved up against the wall. Peanut turns around and lies down in his lap.

⌇

Now there are eight. Nine, counting the dog.

Everyone is back at Bernie's house. He ordered food. Coleman's children aren't saying much, but they've eaten four pizzas between them. Sara nests between her parents on his couch, and Brenda is in the chair with Peanut safe in her lap.

He's skillfully avoided Andrea, getting everyone drinks and making sure they have enough food. Now he's spent ten minutes in the kitchen, leaning his head against the refrigerator door, solitude enveloping him.

They hadn't known if covering the portraits would work. What magic was trapped inside them? But they hadn't destroyed the paintings, only obscured them. Releasing their subjects. Bernie wondered what had happened to the people who weren't in Willow Ridge—where had they gone? Were they free now?

The only thing he wondered about was the survival of the boys after he'd ripped up the photo. Maybe only portraits held the magic. But perhaps Cold had been alive too long. Perhaps his time had come. Or he'd been living so long in that portrait that the demon had taken over, making more like itself.

Bernie doesn't know. He just hopes it's over.

"Hey."

He jumps at the touch of the hand on his back. Andrea's features are soft as she steps up next to him. "You okay, Dad?"

Becky's smile wavers at him. For a second Bernie feels his wife beside him, a fleeting energy, and then she's gone. The smile becomes Andrea's. She's her own person, and he's missed so much.

He rubs a hand over his face. "Yeah, I guess."

"You want a beer?"

Bernie shakes his head. "Not feeling it today."

"Makes sense. It's been a weird one." She leans back on the kitchen island. "I'm sorry I said you couldn't get a dog."

Bernie snorts. "Sorry it was never your business."

Andrea laughs. "We all want you to be happy, you know."

Bernie looks past her into the living room. The ragtag group of investigators and travelers. The people destroyed and traumatized. Some who might build themselves back up and some who might not.

He shrugs. "Why?"

She considers his response for a second. "You mean why we want you to be happy?"

"Yeah. Like happiness isn't the most important thing in the world, is it?"

Andrea looks down and chews on a strand of hair. She works this statement in her mind. He remembers that look on her face in her childhood, her determination to understand everything.

"Maybe not," she says finally. "But I still love you."

Bernie steps toward her. He wraps his arms around her. Time

doesn't stop, but it pauses, and that moment hangs there, in between all the other moments.

"I love you," she says again, into the flannel fabric of his shoulder.

At first he doesn't respond, because of course she has to know. He's loved her since the day he saw her, marveled over her perfect little body, this creature that Becky brought into being. A perfect representation of a future to come. And he is in that future now. "I love you," he says back, inhaling the apple scent of her shampoo.

When she pulls back, he holds her hands and squeezes them, and they are both smiling.

# THE LITTLE MONSTER

The monsters had lived in the lake for centuries. As years and years passed, they remained, satisfied with their tranquil civilization. Once the humans burst onto the scene, everything changed. These new creatures dominated the lake, starting with fishing spears and going all the way out to motorboats.

The monsters were rattled, though they were also curious. They learned to understand human language. Words filtered down into the lake, and the monsters had excellent hearing, so the air didn't blow the talk away. The monsters thought they might forge a bond with the humans, if only they could get the creatures to notice them.

But to the humans, the monsters were a curiosity and nothing more. Humans talked about the monsters, the sightings, the crash of waves around them as they emerged from the water. That was as far as they went, though. There was no talk of contact, no sense of connection.

And so the monsters retreated. *Let humans be what they are,* they thought.

THE WAVEBLADE CLAN lived near the humans' island of Put-in-Bay. The clan observed the water traffic, the ferry crossing from the mainland multiple times a day.

The youngest of them, Larry, liked to swim as close to the shore as he could get. He didn't care if anyone saw him—in fact, he wanted to be seen. His clan was peaceful, but peaceful was boring. Larry wanted more.

"You'll get over this," his mother would say in the language of the lake. "Our existence is simple. You don't have to make things complicated."

Larry wanted to be complicated. If "complicated" meant excitement, drama—all those things a monster could not experience—he would take it.

He began to consider the surface.

Monsters lived in the water. They were mammals, though, and were required to breathe. That meant Larry could survive on land if he could find a way to moisturize. If he wanted to be truly among the humans, though, he would have to walk, or use a wheelchair. Larry had seen these machines, humans pushing each other along the beach walkways. But did humans help each other retrieve items? He could not manipulate objects—not with these ungainly flippers.

The second-youngest creature, Bess, often stayed close to Larry. She was shy and nervous, always fearing she'd be seen. "I don't know why you're so worried," Larry would say. "We're bigger than them. Besides, they're afraid of us."

BESS AND LARRY swam in lazy circles in the shallowest part of the water they could inhabit. Although far from the shore, they could hear. Humans on the beach chattered and splashed. Larry craned his neck up just enough to see. The young ones threw multicolored balls at each other. Some dug in the sand. Another group tossed a white ball across a net. "They seem to like balls," Larry observed. "Have you ever played with a ball, Bess?"

She didn't answer because she was cowering underwater.

He sighed and dipped back down. "Don't you ever think about it? What it would be like?"

Bess's pretty nostrils flared. "Like what?"

"Being human. Having skin." He ducked lower and spun head over flippers.

"We have skin."

"Yeah, but. Different."

She frowned in the way only a monster can frown. "Not really."

Larry popped back up to breathe. He saw them again, the playing people, his gaze catching on their antics each time. Only Bess's nostrils peeked up over the waves. "Do they think about being us?"

It was a good question. "Maybe," he said. "I wouldn't know."

Larry kept paddling. They could never really stop.

LARRY GREW MORE curious as time went on. His life felt so routine and boring. Eat, sleep, talk to other monsters. Every time he stuck his face out to breathe, he felt a longing like he was missing something.

His mother said the humans didn't have anything the monsters didn't. In fact, the humans had it worse. There had been war on the lake generations ago, and though no monsters lived who had seen it, the colony had never forgotten. Red blood stained the water as human bodies flew from their tall ships. The lake had smelled like rot for weeks.

"We have beautiful lives here," his mother said. "Why would you want more than this?"

He didn't understand why he had to answer this question, why he had to apologize for his desires. Why he couldn't wonder about possibilities.

There had always been rumors, although he had never taken them to heart or cared whether they were true. There were lake serpents far below, who didn't need to breathe, who practiced magical rituals. Maybe one of them could change him, or at least help him learn about what he was missing. Because he knew something was, even if his mother said he was wrong. The creatures on the surface shone, laughed, cried. Their emotions ran deeper than the lake.

He did the math. He could stay underwater for about thirty minutes before he had to go back up. It wasn't enough time. He might get lost or fail to convince the serpents to give him what he wanted. He might not be able to explain himself. They could look at him like he had lost his mind and put a spell on him to keep him quiet.

But anything could happen, truly. And if he didn't try, he would regret it.

He checked with Bessie before he left. She wouldn't go with him, of course, but he asked her if she could swim in the general area where he would descend.

At his question, she drew in a plume of water, then stuck her head up and coughed.

"No." She pulled her head down and fixed him with a decidedly non-Bessie-like stare. "I am not letting you go there."

"Last time I checked, it wasn't your decision." Larry felt a cold current pass below him. "I need you to cover for me."

She appeared stricken and didn't respond.

"I'll get you some of the good seaweed from the bottom," he said. "And there are probably fish down there."

"How would you even know that?" she sputtered. "How do I know you'll make it back?"

"You don't," Larry said.

LARRY WENT DOWN and down and down until he reached the bottom of the lake. His flippers grazed the wet soil.

This was no ocean, although Larry would not have known an ocean existed or what it was. There were no caves for him to explore, no witches hiding in crevices. The water was murky, and Larry squinted into the deep. "Hello?"

If the rumors weren't true, and there was no one here, he would simply rise to the surface and forget this ever happened. But as Larry navigated the darkness, he felt a new emptiness in his body. Without this hope, he had nothing to think about. Nothing to dream for. He would have to envision a new dream, and that thought made him anxious.

He called out for a few minutes, the sound centered in the bottom of his throat.

He was about to turn around and go back when he heard a noise in the distance. It was so thin and quiet that he couldn't tell exactly where it came from. "Hello?" he called out again.

"Come here," said the voice, louder this time.

Larry drifted closer.

The lake serpent emerged. She was tiny, only a few feet long, and she swam in spirals as if she could never stop moving. Her voice remained small, but he was close enough to hear her now. "What do you wish for?" she asked.

"Why are you here?" He peered at her. "Why do you do this? Rather than live among us."

"You are full of questions." She was moving so fast that he couldn't see her face, but he thought he got a glint of a snakelike eye. "This is the path of all serpents."

"But why is this your path?"

"My existence does not concern you." The serpent paused in her circling. "What do you want?"

Larry's chest tightened, a reminder that he did not have long. "I want to visit the surface."

"Of course you do."

"Is that what everyone wants?"

The serpent laughed and began swimming again, more lazily now. "I am not at liberty to disclose that."

"Can you do it?"

She drew closer to him. Her circles tightened around his neck until he thought she'd take the breath out of his body. Her tiny mouth brushed against his ear. "I can do anything. For a price."

Monsters did not have a concept of money (which could become a problem later) but Larry understood the idea of trading valuables. He needed to sacrifice for this chance. "What can I do for you?" he asked.

"You are going to the surface."

"Yes."

The serpent fell back, eyeing Larry straight on, a hint of sadness in her voice. "I want you to find someone."

LARRY FOUND Bessie dozing as she floated above the waves. Night had fallen, and the moon cast white light on the water. She was so relaxed that he didn't want to disturb her.

But she must have noticed his excitement. "You're back?" she asked with her eyes still closed.

"Bess, this is going to be freaking amazing." He clutched two bottom-growing plants in one flipper. As flippers are not meant to carry objects, it had been difficult, but he had not lost them. "We're going up. We're going to be among people."

She looked at him askance. "We?"

"Yeah! She gave me two doses. I told her I didn't want to go out there alone."

"But you didn't ask me."

Larry gaped. "I thought you would want to come."

"I didn't even want you to go to the sea serpent." Her jaw began to shake. "All this is scaring me."

Larry's flipper was beginning to ache. He needed to eat these plants or let them go. But he had promised the lake serpent that he would find the man she wanted. He told Bessie so.

"So you'll do what she wants, but not what I want. Which is to stay here and not mess with the natural order of things."

"I thought you wanted to go!" Larry nearly threw up his flippers, but he thought better at the last moment. "You said you were thinking about what the surface would be like."

Bess turned from him, faced the other direction. "Thinking is not the same as doing."

LARRY SWAM as far up to the shore as he could. He found a stone formation and awkwardly slid in the extra dose. If Bess wouldn't take it, he'd find someone who would appreciate it.

He held his breath for a moment before popping the herb into his mouth. It tasted no different from the seaweed he normally ate. He felt no different, either. Could the lake snake be a fraud? No, Larry thought. She wanted him to find someone, a very specific person. She wouldn't trick him.

A few more minutes went by before it started.

Larry grimaced as his flippers began to elongate. Pain lit up his entire body. His throat closed, and he struggled to breathe. Human hands sprouted from human wrists. Human ankles gave way to human feet. Larry blacked out.

When he came to, he was floating near the sand. He took bumbling steps onto the shore.

He steadied himself by grabbing onto a tree. It felt rough under his new hands. The skin was pink and thin, not like the leathery hide he was used to. The feet were the same way, heels pressing into hot sand.

Humans—*people*, his mind said—gathered down the beach. It was early, the sun on its way up the sky. They carried blankets, coolers, umbrellas. Planning to spend an entire day lying there. Larry ran the hands up and down the arms. The skin felt vulnerable under the light, as if the sun might crisp him to death.

He didn't have clothes. Not even the skimpy shorts and bathing suits the people wore. Monsters didn't have to worry about covering themselves. Even if they wanted to decorate themselves, they could not, not with the garments humans chose. The fabric would get wet. Larry wanted to see what those items would feel like on the skin. He wanted every sensation, every new feeling.

Maybe someone up the beach would give him clothes. On careful steps, he set out toward the closest set of humans.

He assessed them: large one, small one, even smaller one. Their skin was darker than his, browner. The small one had dark curly hair that fell down her back. The other two had short cropped hair. The biggest one had an impressive set of muscles.

"Excuse me," he began.

Everyone in the family froze. The small one gasped, dropped her blanket. She talked, but Larry didn't understand her. Then she shrieked and went running down the beach. The taller one looked between the small one and the even smaller one, then seemed to decide that he should stay with the even smaller one. Larry thought this may have been a young human, unable to be left alone, like the pups in his pod.

The even smaller human stared up at Larry. It squeaked out some words Larry didn't understand.

The big human stared too but didn't say anything.

Larry knew when he was not wanted, but his new chest felt tight anyway. He moved the fingers, waggled them, and they clenched up of their own will. They were rigid, difficult to move. Made of bones.

He turned and wobbled away.

Larry concealed himself behind a leafy tree, finding a spot in the shade. He needed to find a person who could communicate with him. He missed Bess.

But the humans' screaming had made him wary. Larry had never seen the humans so close, but he could sense their fear.

Larry lowered his neck and circled it around his body. He laid his head on the grass and examined the new feeling. Tiny blades raked up and down his leathery cheek. The hands and fingers couldn't settle, but his face was familiar. It was still his.

He must have fallen asleep, because when he looked up, the sky was red and purple, the horizon awash in sunset. Larry scanned the beach—no humans in sight. He was alone now.

Back on the new feet, Larry continued to stumble, but he felt more confident as his soles slapped the sand. The shore was no longer warm. He was shivering, a new experience, shoulders shaking with cold.

This might have been a mistake. But it was only the first day. So he was optimistic. He could figure out a plan.

"Hey!"

A voice called out from the lake. A voice he knew and understood.

"Bess?" he called back.

"I wanted to check on you." She was close to the shore, but she couldn't get to the shallowest areas, and they were yelling back and forth. "I couldn't let you be out here all alone."

"So get out here with me!" Larry stumbled his way down the beach. "I still have that extra dose."

Her head poked out from above the water. "I don't know about that."

"Please. We can figure this out together."

Bess didn't respond. Larry heard the bleat of a ferry horn from nearby.

"Bess, please. I need someone to talk to. No one understands me here." He swallowed. "They're scared of me."

She laughed. "Of course they are."

"Why? I have a body like theirs. It is so weird, by the way. You should try it."

"Larry, since you can't see me, I'll tell you I'm rolling my eyes."

Larry stomped one of the feet. He never would have thought to do that, but the angry gesture felt like part of his new DNA. He lost his balance and fell on his behind, the bones there smarting. "I don't understand any of this!"

"You still look like us," Bess said. "They have different heads."

Larry was breathing hard from the fall. "I know you, Bess! You're thinking about it!"

"Okay, okay! I am!" Bess yelled back. "It's lonely without you."

"Then take it!" Larry cupped his hands around his mouth, and the sound traveled straight to her. "I put the stuff in a cove near the shallows. I'll wait."

～

MORNING CAME, but Bess wasn't there.

Larry had to go to the other side of the island to watch the sunrise. He'd found a beach towel and wrapped it around his torso for warmth. It was still unbearably cold, but he was so curious, and he didn't want to waste time.

And he had to find the human for the lake serpent. That was part of the deal. If Larry didn't find the human, the lake serpent would never give him the herb to change back into a monster. Being a human with a monster head would not be fun, especially if he could not communicate with anyone.

The human lived on the island. He was white, tall, with a gray beard and a barrel chest. The serpent had last seen him in what she called a restaurant. "It's where humans sit down and eat," she'd said. "They have many more choices than we do. It's really not fair." The human was male and worked at the restaurant, but she'd met with him at a table late at night, having taken the herb herself. He spoke the language of the lake—he was the only human that she had truly connected with.

As Larry walked along the island's main street, he studied each restaurant. One had a long pier that extended into the lake. The others were on the land side near a bunch of buildings. Larry had never seen any of these structures before, and he marveled at the architecture. He had no idea what kind of civilizations these humans had built. They had so much more than the dark water.

He'd have to search the restaurants. This would present a problem, he thought as he considered his excuse for clothing, not to mention his monster head.

Larry suddenly felt very tired. He was fascinated by everything here, by the body he wore now, but he was running low on solutions. Soon the humans would be awake, people would be outside walking down this street, and everyone would be scared of him. He collapsed onto a green bench, letting his legs rest.

He stared straight ahead, taking in the sights around him before he had to return to the woods. A squat building stood across from him. Racks of clothing were displayed in the window. This must be where the humans got them.

After resting for a few more moments, he got up and approached the place. He peeked into the window. There were all kinds of garments, although none that he would recognize, and none that he would know how to wear. The towel slipped on his hips, and he wrenched it back up as he thought.

A garment caught his eye, far to the left of his vision. He turned his neck to see an image of... himself. There were squiggles that indicated water, and a profile of a long neck stuck out. And there were squiggles below it. Larry had never seen written language, so he did not know that the words read *Lake Erie Monsters.*

LARRY DIDN'T KNOW how money worked on the surface. He didn't know how to get into the store, nor did he know it was called a store. He did know two things:

1. Anything he did would scare the humans.
2. He needed clothes.

He reasoned that people also needed clothes and that they could get inside. So there must be for him to enter.

He continued sitting on the bench as the sun rose higher. He was thirsty but determined. And his instincts proved true: as people wandered out into the street, blinking in the sunlight, they saw him and gasped. Screamed. Ran away.

A new feeling rose inside him. He was pleased. If they wouldn't accept him, they could fear him. And that wasn't so bad.

Larry leaned into his discomfort. He let his greatest bellows loose. He found his footing and ran, enjoying the power in his new legs, the strange genitals between them bouncing. His plan—to get the clothes out of the store—collapsed and turned into ash. Larry didn't need it anymore. He was still himself even though he wore a different body.

HE CUT through the wooded area that abutted the beach, where he'd been hiding. When he hit the sand, in full view of the humans there, a roar came from the crowd. The screams were music, pulsing in his ears. He ran down to the end of the beach where the water was deeper and plunged his face into it. It was cool. He lapped it up, letting it rush into his body like medicine.

Larry was breathing hard. Breath was different in this body. The lungs were so much smaller. He pulled his head out of the water and sucked in air.

He returned to the grass, where he'd felt that sweet sensation of touch, and lay down. He hadn't realized how sore the body was. It wasn't the kind of fatigue he experienced as a monster. The muscles were different, strained different. Land was hard under these fragile feet. Larry had a lake full of buoyancy that soothed him when he ached.

This was useless, he thought. None of this was for him. He didn't belong here.

Gradually, he noticed movement around him. In bushes, behind trees. Of course, Larry did not know what a cell phone was, nor could he understand the concept. But these were indeed phones, people reaching out from behind natural features, trying to get a glimpse of Larry.

He could smell them, though, and sensed them there. Anger blew through him like a wind, hot at first but then cooling and gone. Larry didn't have the energy to be tired. He wanted to go home.

"Larry?"

He jerked his head up, his long neck unfurling. A human stood right in front of him, speaking the language of the monsters. Slowly, other humans gathered around the man, flanking him, and Larry's skin crawled. He would be outnumbered.

"Yes," Larry said. "Who are you?"

"My name is Hodel," he replied.

Larry blinked. This was the person he had been charged to find. And now the human was here, right in front of him. He hadn't had to search at all.

But he had done something. He had run down that street, showed the humans he was there and that he was different. That he had become some bizarre hybrid, neither human nor monster. This must have drawn Hodel out. The one the lake serpent had been looking for.

"You're here to help me." Larry rose to his feet. "She wants you."

"Her name is Mazaar."

Larry felt a twinge. He hadn't even thought to ask her. "Mazaar asked me to find you in exchange for experiencing the island."

Hodel nodded. He was a small man, not nearly as tall as Larry, especially with Larry's head snaking up into the air. He wore a green cargo jacket and shorts, and he was mostly bald, with small round glasses perched on his nose. "And so you have, and you can return to the lake."

Larry felt sick.

Hodel tilted his head. "You don't want to."

"I don't know." Larry raised a hand to his face, drew the palm down his cheek. "It would be different if..."

"You didn't eat enough of the plant."

"What?"

"You consumed half a dose. You didn't change all the way." Hodel moved forward, and Larry cringed. Hodel put out his palms. "It's okay. It was an honest mistake."

"I hid the rest. For Bess."

"You want to go back for her?"

Larry's shoulders slumped. "I may as well."

The people around Hodel continued holding their cell phones up. Taking video of this tremendous conversation, the man and the creature howling at each other.

"What's your name?" Hodel asked softly.

"Larry."

"And your love?"

Larry tilted his head. "I don't love her."

Hodel stepped forward again. This time Larry didn't wince. Hodel came close to him, touched his arm. The feeling of human skin against skin was new, soft. A connection despite the fragility.

"You may want to think about that," the man said.

"If she cared about me, she would have come."

"You write your own stories, my son." Hodel's hand moved to Larry's shoulder. "Her decision wasn't yours. Do you see Mazaar here?"

Larry didn't know how to answer.

Hodel reached in his pocket and held out a plant. It looked similar to the one Larry had ingested earlier. "You are tired, hungry, thirsty. Now was not the right time for you to be here. But this doesn't mean you are exiled forever, Larry. The earth is always here for you."

Larry grabbed the plant and sucked it into his mouth.

"Go!" Hodel yelled as he stepped back. "It won't be long!"

HE HURTLED DOWN the shore and into the water. The arms were changing already, lowering, widening. The legs, too, shortened into the paddles he was used to. Larry's flippers skimmed the lake floor until he could get himself into deeper water. He plunged his head down and let the waves roll around him, the feel of it revitalizing him.

"Bess!" he called. "Bess!"

She swam up from below. "There you are! I'm so glad you're back."

Maybe he imagined the joy in her voice. "Me too."

"What was it like up there?"

He sighed. "Not what I expected."

She was still swimming, circling him. They were always on the move in the lake, twirling through the water in an endless dance. "What did you expect?"

"I don't know. They were scared of me. I couldn't connect with them." Larry cast a glance down into the dirty depths. "She did, though. Mazaar."

"Who's that?"

"The lake serpent. She wanted me to find that man—remember?"

Bess shook her long neck. Larry's gaze traced it up and down before he realized what he was doing. "That was all quite confusing. I was worried you'd never come home."

Larry felt strange. "I know."

LARRY WAS MORE RESTED as night approached. He'd had a nap, some seaweed, and a few walleye, not to mention gulps and gulps of water. And night was the most beautiful, the best part of being a monster. Moonlight reflecting on the waves, a soft serenity engulfing them. No boats, no horns, no humans.

He was staring out at the land when Bess glided up beside him. "What are you thinking?"

"Not much, honestly." It was like he'd lost something–that burning ache to be on land, to experience new feelings. That hope was gone now, his purpose evaporated.

"Do you want to go up to the shore?" She sounded almost shy.

He hesitated. He didn't really. But her liquid eyes caught his, and he wanted to make her happy.

They cruised out as far as they could go, although this was still quite far. He remembered standing on the beach and calling out to Bess, wanting her to be beside him. How sad he was when she wouldn't come.

Beside him, Bess gasped.

It was hard to tell, but Larry was sure the man standing on the beach was Hodel. He wore that same green jacket, and light glinted off his bald head. The man stood with his arms spread, and the monsters could hear him, understand him. "Mazaar!" he called out.

A human stepped from the waves. She was tiny, shapely, her hips swaying as she moved toward Hodel. Her hair was long and shiny, the color of seaweed, and she wore no clothes. Larry was transfixed as she stepped into his arms. Hodel's hand went to her back. The humans pressed their lips together, and Larry wondered why.

"I didn't try that," he said to Bess. "I didn't have lips."

The woman's feet were unsteady. Hodel wrapped his arms around her shoulders and helped her up the beach and into the woods.

Bess turned to him. "I... don't know what to say."

Larry leaned in, closer than he'd ever been. "You don't have to say a thing."

# EXIT THROUGH THE GIFT SHOP

Why did we think the zoo was a good idea? *Fun activities for kids,* the Internet said. Right. Because wrangling screaming kids from car seats to strollers is fun.

There isn't much to do with a two-year-old and a six-month-old. Sean and I prided ourselves on getting out of the house regularly. I'd wear the baby in a carrier on my front, making sure he was close enough to kiss, silently judging the people who let their kids sag too low. But we were far from perfect parents, as evidenced by the current hell that was wresting Betsy and August from the Subaru Outback.

"Don' wanna!" Betsy's pink cheeks were streaked with tears. She was rigid in my arms, wedged between her seat and the door.

"We could have just gone to Target," Sean said as he lifted August from his rear-facing bucket seat. August was more mewling than screaming, his face red, and I had a feeling I would be changing a diaper once we found a bathroom.

"But this is a *fun activity for children,*" I pointed out.

I moved back from Betsy so Sean could hand me the baby. I was already wearing the carrier across my front, deflated as if I was carrying an invisible child. Sean handed me the baby. I received August, wrapped him in the front panel of the carrier, and lifted the backpack-

like straps over my shoulders. A foul smell wafted up, and I tried not
to gag.

Sean, meanwhile, coerced Betsy out of her seat by promising ice
cream. "It's that easy??" I yelled. Now I was Bad Mommy while Sean
was the golden parent. I pictured a teenage Betsy running to her dad
after I told her she couldn't buy whatever the future stupid thing of the
moment was. He'd cave. Maybe August would like me better.

AT LEAST IT was a small zoo. It only took us an hour or so to complete
the circle. Betsy strained out of her stroller, so we let her go out and
run, only to have her disappear and Sean go pelting after her.

August, now clean, began whimpering. I found a bench near the
otter enclosure and removed him from the carrier to nurse. I never
used a cover, preferring to stare daggers at anyone who whispered
about what I was doing. There had been a whole thing with a woman
in a restaurant who said she didn't want to see "that" while she was
eating. I said, "Well, he needs to eat too." I got kicked out, so my fellow
breastfeeding people from La Leche League staged a nurse-in. It was
amazing.

Sean turned the corner back to us, toting Betsy. She now looked
more rueful than angry, her blue eyes narrowed to slits, curly golden
hair all mussed. "Did you know they have a cryptid exhibit?" Sean
asked.

"Huh?"

"Yeah. Like Bigfoot?"

"Bigfoot isn't real." I burped the baby and got him reset on my front.
"Is it like an informational thing? Except with, like, fake news?"

Sean shook his head. His curls were more auburn, and I wondered
if my children's hair would one day darken to that shade. "No, like real
enclosures."

I scoffed. "No way."

"C'mon." He came to me and took my hand, hoisting me up. "Betsy
ran right into it."

"No Mothman, Daddy!" she crowed. "No Mothman!"

"We won't stay long." Sean rubbed his hand over her hair. "I want to show Mommy."

"No Mommy!" yelled Betsy. My heart tugged, but I nestled my face in August's hair, breathing in his soft baby scent. Which was much better now that we'd jettisoned the diaper.

I waved a hand. "I don't have to look. It's okay."

I was curious, though. My brain didn't often have time to churn through adult thoughts. I'd never really considered cryptids as a thing. I knew of their existence, but they were only silly myths. Single people like my brother had time to research and decide on their reality. I was too busy chasing Betsy and tending to August. They were my whole life. But inside me, there was an adult, and she wanted to see what this was all about.

Sean put Betsy back in her stroller. She squalled for a bit but then turned her head to the side and conked out. August was asleep too, milk-drunk. Yes, we were those asshole parents who didn't give our kids proper naps. It was too much work to spend an hour coaxing them to sleep only to have them wake up thirty minutes later.

The cryptid exhibit was up ahead. We slowed down, taking every second to savor the quiet. There were no other kids racing around: only us, viewing the empty areas.

A zoo attendant in a blue polo stood in front of a glass pane, her hair in box braids, her skin a warm brown. Her name tag read *Jasmine.* She was young—I was jealous of her clear skin and wide-awake eyes. "Hello!" she called out. "Welcome to Cryptid Carnival!"

"Hi," I said, summoning enthusiasm so she could tell I was more than a mom. Somewhere inside, I was still cool. "This is new, huh?"

She nodded. "Honestly, it's way better if you come at night. For the adults-only viewings. You can see a lot more."

"But how do you even—how do you catch them?" Sean asked, pointing to the information plaque about the chupacabra. "Don't they, like, drink blood?"

"They're sweeter than you think. Well, at least some of them."

Jasmine indicated a person walking down the hill toward us. "That's my boss, Destiny. She handles the evening shift, feedings and stuff."

Destiny was white, her short brown hair streaked with green. She had a septum piercing and ears adorned all the way up. She joined us, her polo rippling as she stretched. "Sorry," she said to us. "Still waking up. Not a lot to see, but what do you think? Would you come back for the night show?"

I traded a glance with Sean. I would. But there was the matter of babysitting. We couldn't afford even the rates from the teens in our neighborhood, and both our families lived hours away. I turned away and saw bushy antennae peeking up from behind a rock.

I blinked and stepped back. "Oh my God."

The Mothman raised its head and looked straight at me. Daring me somehow. It raised huge wings and began beating them without breaking eye contact.

Betsy stirred. Blinked. She raised her head, saw it, and immediately began shrieking. "No Mothman!"

"Thank you!" I yelled to the zoo staff while we hurried away. But I could still see that creature, its gaze holding mine as if trying to drill the tender tissue of my brain.

THE GIFT SHOP boasted a rack of plush otters, bears, tigers. Betsy coveted them until she saw the red-eyed Mothmen. We were out of there like bats from hell. I said a silent thank you to the universe for saving me from a fight with a two-year-old over a stuffy.

Later that evening, when the kids were temporarily asleep, Sean and I turned on *Star Trek: The Next Generation* and zoned out. It was a comfort show from my childhood, always on in the next room while I fell asleep. My parents were nerds, into every space show and super-hero movie, but *TNG* was the only one that made me feel cared for.

"Ew," Sean said. "It's the one where they turn into dinosaurs."

I couldn't remember why the crew had devolved, but I could still see Troi's gills and her mouth flapping like a fish's. "Ew. Should we switch the channel?"

"Nah. It's weird but cool."

"Ugh, the CGI is so outdated." I rested my head on the back of the couch. "I should turn in."

"Just sit with me for a while. You can rest." Sean picked up a foot and began kneading it. I groaned. The massage was soothing against my tired skin.

I dozed until an image flashed against the darkness behind my lids. *Red. Antennae. Wings.*

When I startled awake, the Troi scene was on, and I clasped at my neck as if I too could not breathe.

"Daph? Are you okay?" Sean was kneeling next to me now, his hands on my arm instead of my feet. "What's wrong?"

"It's just…" *Wings. Red. Antennae.* "Could we go to that cryptid show? After dark?"

Sean blinked. "You really want to do that?"

"Can we? I'm curious."

He frowned as he trailed his hand down my arm. "I guess. Think you could pick up a couple hours at the shop? For the sitter."

I occasionally worked at a crunchy, natural baby store in town when the owner needed someone on short notice. "Yeah, I'll check with Joan if you don't mind watching Betsy a couple nights."

"It's not 'watching' her. Since I'm her parent and all." Sean smiled, and goosebumps prickled along my skin.

As promised, I worked the hours. Joan, mother to thirteen (!) children, was gracious enough to let me come in even when the other employees were there. She said she could use help cleaning the place: folding little shirts, arranging cloth diapers, dusting shelves filled with breast pumps and nipple-emulating bottles. "For women who work," the packages read. "Your baby is precious even when you're away."

"So you're having some adult time." Joan leaned her elbows on the register table and sighed. "That must be nice."

"I think it will be." August snoozed on my front in a colorful ring sling, one I'd bought here with my employee discount. "I haven't been away from the kids since before Betsy was born."

Joan nodded. She had wan skin, almost green, and I could see the hard years in the lines on her face. Her hair was dyed a bright red, but I knew there was stark white behind it.

"You should enjoy it," Joan said. "What are you doing again?"

"It's weird. Don't judge me?"

She laughed lightly. "Nothing you can say would surprise me."

"The zoo has a cryptid exhibit. Like, Bigfoot? Creatures."

True to her word, she did not seem fazed. "Not weird at all."

"But how do they even catch them?"

Bells above the door chimed, signaling the arrival of a customer. A heavily pregnant woman sauntered in.

Joan said, "There are ways."

She walked to the front and greeted the woman, her voice smooth with years of experience, asking how she could help. I faced the window too, patting August's back, looking through the glass at the parking lot past it.

JOAN'S oldest daughter agreed to watch the kids for us. She was a statuesque fortysomething, freckles sprinkled along her nose, light red hair long and curling gently at the ends. "Do you have kids?" I asked her, making small talk as she took off her coat and slipped off her shoes.

She shook her head. "Been single my whole life. But I'm the cool aunt to many."

I chuckled. "I imagine with that many siblings, you've got lots of experience."

"That's an understatement."

Judy followed me to our bedroom to meet August and then Betsy, who was playing with blocks in her room. We needed a bigger space for sure, but we didn't have the money and I was unsure if we ever would. The kids would have to share a room, as awkward as it would be for siblings. Maybe by puberty Sean would be making more money, or I'd get a job. Maybe take over the shop. Maybe I could become an old-lady model for JC Penney, rocking stonewashed mom jeans and a V-neck sweater.

Sean came out of the bathroom in a hoodie and jeans as I was showing Judy where my pumped milk was. "I nursed him half an hour ago, so you probably won't need it, but just in case," I said. "Is there anything else you need to know? Which blankets they like? Betsy will need a diaper change before she goes to sleep. Augie might wake up a few times. He's not good at staying down—"

Judy patted me on the back. "Don't worry, Daphne. It will be okay."

THE SKY WAS SPITTING, a sort of snow-like rain. The main zoo was all lit up, purple lights strung along path railings and abstract metal sculptures. It was past St. Patrick's Day, but our guide told us the display would be up through the beginning of April. "Lights aren't only for Christmas," she told us. "They're fun. The kids will have an Easter egg hunt later in the month too."

The guide was familiar, and I realized she was Destiny, the boss of the attendant we'd met outside the Mothman's habitat. She was the expert, I remembered. "It'll be a quick tour through here," she announced as we trooped through the main zoo. "You'll notice we have some new animals since last season."

"Not that we would know," Sean whispered, his breath tickling the shell of my ear.

For once in our lives, we were adult humans. We marveled at the swans curled up to sleep, the tigers stalking in their lit-up enclosure. The zoo was different at night. Some animals wanted no part of it, while others perked up. I was sure the lights were messing with their circadian rhythms.

Destiny announced that there was a minibar station available before we moved on to the next part of the tour. Sean grabbed a beer, but I shook my head.

"You can pump and dump. Or even nurse. I don't think Augie would notice a trace of wine in your milk." He elbowed me. "You've gotta relax a little, babe."

My lips clamped shut. Relaxing was not a thing. Even if I could be an adult for a few hours, I couldn't forget my children, how much they needed me. Sean shrugged and enjoyed his beverage.

As everyone milled about, drinks in hand, Destiny stood at the front of the line and clapped. "All right, everyone! We're heading into the cryptid exhibits now. I'll remind you that no other zoo on the planet has a tour like this. It will be completely dark. You're welcome to use the flashlights on your phones, but please point them at the ground. The creatures will not come out if they feel they're being threatened."

A few phones lit up. Sean squeezed my hand. "You ready?" he whispered.

A traveling tram pulled into the holding area. This would take us through this part of the zoo, as if we were going on a hayride. Sean and I hoisted each other up in tandem. We settled on a cold seat that felt like a bleacher. I winced at the spots of water that sank into the behind of my jeans.

Once everyone was aboard, the tram started and began to roll forward. I wasn't nervous, just curious. But my heart picked up speed regardless.

Destiny cleared her throat. "First, we'll encounter the storied Bigfoot, also known as Sasquatch. That's right, folks, we've captured one of these majestic creatures, which roams in the forests of the Pacific Northwest. There are plenty of Sasquatch in our area, though, especially north of here and moving up into the Canadian forest. The name comes from an indigenous people, but every culture had a different name for the beast."

No one was listening. They were peering into the pen, craning for a glimpse. Sean had turned his entire body and was searching.

"There it is!" someone yelled.

A huge hominid crashed through the wooded area and sprang into view. Since it was so dark, we could only see its outline. But we sure heard the roar, an ear-piercing cry on par with a lion's. I shrank back into Sean's arms. The creature grumbled and stalked away.

"Aren't you lucky you got a glimpse of him?" Destiny beamed. "Next up, the Fresno Nightcrawlers. Not much is known about these creatures. They are white or gray with no arms and very long legs. A man in Fresno caught one on a fuzzy outdoor camera, which led to their name. But they have been seen in many other places, including right here in Ohio. Which is where we found these sweet friends!"

The next area was a meadow. Two large bushes were set apart in the back, and we could see the Nightcrawlers running between them, surrounded by an ethereal glow.

Even in the darkness, I could see Sean rolling his eyes. "I shoulda known," he muttered.

The meadow's fence was low—too low to keep the creatures in. The Nightcrawlers were decidedly fake, on some kind of revolving contraption so they could be seen from far away. Tiny spotlights next to each tree highlighted the figures.

My heartbeat slowed. "Honestly, it's a relief."

Sean grinned and wrapped me tighter. All his familiar scents breathed into my skin. This was the closest to relaxed I could get. "Were you scared?"

"A little," I admitted.

Destiny took us through the history of the Chupacabra, the Wendigo, and even the Yeti. The Yeti's pen was fully enclosed, fake snow drifting from its ceiling, an elaborate icy landscape designed for our entertainment. The supposed Yeti was snoozing next to a frozen-over lake.

The last pen was the most ridiculous yet. Spooky sounds and spotlights played over a display in the middle. "Yes, this is possibly the rarest cryptid you've ever seen," Destiny said, clearly trying not to laugh. "This is the Ghost of the XBOX Kinect. That's right, folks, this outdated piece of gaming equipment can illuminate ghosts as they pass through the air. The motion sensor technology gets them right on camera." She pointed to an old TV screen behind the Kinect, which portrayed a series of distorted images.

"I hate to say this," Sean said, "but I'm excited to get home."

I didn't know how to feel. Being apart from the kids tore me in two, but I had craved this alone time. Yet I wasn't even alone—Sean was with me. Would I ever hear silence again?

The tram chugged to a stop, and the participants began to depart. I could see why the zoo had installed the minibar before the tour.

We turned around and headed toward the parking lot. Sean said, "Hey, we didn't see Mothman."

I froze. "Oh, that's okay. We saw it before."

"We could at least take another look?" He winked. "At least to see what kind of animatronics they've got in there."

I'd almost forgotten about those red eyes. At the mention of them, I found myself losing breath again.

The Mothman enclosure was situated just outside the gift shop, in the opposite direction of the tour. "I wonder why we didn't go past it," Sean mused. "You'd think the guide would be hot to trot on that mythology."

"People do love Mothman," I murmured.

We arrived. Sean tapped on the glass, and I hissed—well, benevo-lently—at him. "What?" he shot back.

"I don't think the zookeepers would like you doing that."

He scoffed. "Yeah, for this totally fake exhibit, I have to be so careful."

"Glass is glass. You break it, you bought it."

"Like I'm gonna break this entire glass pane with one fingernail." He held up a hand. "And a stubby fingernail at that."

"Okay, okay." I retreated. It wasn't worth it to start a fight.

But Sean didn't seem fazed. "I don't know why you always have to be so critical. Like every time I change the baby the way you don't like, or how I swaddle him. Like how I let Betsy watch too many screens."

It was best to not engage. But I felt rage screaming up through the middle of my body, that body that no longer belonged to me.

"It makes me feel like a bad parent," Sean continued.

"You think you're a bad parent?" I leaned up closer to the glass myself, avoiding making eye contact. "You get to leave every day for hours on end. I'm the one rotting Betsy's brain all day while I'm trying to take care of Augie."

He leaned on the glass, one elbow perching him at an angle. "You've got their naptimes."

"Because our kids are ace at lying down for naps."

Sean sighed. "Well, there's nothing in here. Just another con. Let's go. This place is for the kids."

He walked away from me, but I kept staring. I willed myself to see it. I don't know what I was trying to prove. That the zoo wasn't totally bullshit, I guess. Or that I hadn't been wrong, and what I saw was real, not some animatronic nonsense.

There were lights here, projecting from the path onto the ground. The creature could not be fully nocturnal since I'd seen it during the day. I hoped I wasn't disturbing it. *I just want to see you,* I thought. *Please. One minute of your time.* As if I was a cold-caller trying to sell some product to a bemused executive.

"Daphne? Where are you?" Sean yelled. Awesome that he didn't notice I was gone for so long.

I was about to turn and leave when I caught the glimpse. Bushy antennae again, those red eyes peeking at me from behind a plant. My heart caught in my throat, and I waved.

The creature stepped toward me. I couldn't believe what I was seeing. How could the zoo hold this back from its guests? To preserve the sense of spectacle they'd created with their tour? Destiny was supposed to be the expert, but we'd only talked to her about Mothman when we'd visited with the kids. This connection between us—it was a secret. Something only I shared with it.

Below the creature, there was a murmur of sound and activity. More red eyes peeking out at me. They were behind the creature's legs. Scared—of me?

She wasn't a Mothman after all. And these were her children.

We locked eyes again, and she understood. I understood. The message hung in the air between us.

THE KIDS WERE asleep when we relieved Judy, but no sooner than an hour after we got home, Augie was up again. I nursed him in bed while drifting off. Then Betsy was awake: a dirty diaper. Sean was snoring. An hour later, Augie again.

I managed to patch together a few hours of sleep after I fed the baby for the second time. Both kids were awake and screaming by six. Sean groaned and rolled over. I ground my teeth and rolled out of bed.

When Sean woke up, both kids were riveted by Baby Mozart. I patted myself on the back for keeping them educated.

"Hey. You mad?" He curled his arms around me. It wasn't like last night, when he smelled like our past, like our life before the kids. Now his breath was sour and ugly. I didn't answer him.

"Daphne?"

I spit out the first response that came to me. "I have to go."

He spun me to look at him, his eyes wide. "Go where?"

"I don't know."

"Why?"

I grabbed my car keys off the kitchen counter. "I don't know."

The morning was crisp and cold, but I breathed it in like it was summer air. I jumped into the Subaru and started it up. Backed out of the driveway. My car was pointed toward the freeway, so I aimed for it. I didn't know where I would go or how long I'd be gone, but I knew I would return; I knew I could not leave my children forever. But now? Now was a different story.

I tuned the radio to the nineties pop station and sang along. Semisonic came on: "Closing Time." I didn't have to go home, and I wasn't staying there.

# CLEARANCE HAMSTER

This all started because Tim had to have a betta to replace the dead one. He couldn't go a day without having a fish in the tank by his bed. "Don't you want to grieve Axel?" I asked him as we hiked through the parking lot to the pet store. "You're going to replace him the very same day?"

Tim stopped, turned, and sent an eyebrow up to his curly hairline. "Of course I'm going to grieve Axel. But I need a new fish to comfort me."

I rolled my eyes as he turned and kept walking. Grieving, my ass. We'd had to go to Famous Footwear before we came here since he needed a "consolation gift." I said nothing while my roommate forked over a hundred bucks for a pair of cherry-red Converse. Wished I had that kind of money, but at least Tim provided me shelter. I had a roof over my pretty blond head, thrifted clothes on my body, and I could eat whatever leftovers I brought home from the bakery. Although by now, I consisted completely of carbs.

And Tim wasn't the type to flaunt his wealth. Thin with a closely cropped 'fro and an easy smile, he exuded joy no matter where he went. He was always dressed either impeccably, in a tailored suit and wingtips, or totally flamboyantly, in a myriad of colors and textures. He was always light on his feet, the bounce in his step ever-present. And I could always use a dose of that sunshine.

Goosebumps rose on my arms as we entered the store. "Do they keep frozen pets in here?" I asked. "Like, they pull 'em out of the back and thaw 'em for sale?"

Tim didn't have time to reply. We bumped into a barricade: an employee in her bright blue apron. She had smoke lines around her lips and orange hair of a shade not found in nature. Her name tag read GLENDA.

"Can I help you?" Her voice was a growl.

"Oh no, no." I hoped she hadn't heard me talking about the frozen animals. "We're good. Thank you, though!"

Tim and I sailed away on light feet toward the fish area. "Do you think she was one of the pets?" I asked him.

"Oh my God, Katy." Tim put his slab of a hand over his face. "You are going to get us kicked out of here."

I propped my hands on my hips. "Guess we'd have to go to Meijer for a fish then."

Tim pouted. "I mean, it's legit that we would go and save them from their impending doom. But they die so fast. Like, I had just gotten to know Stevie when he passed. You know, the one before Axel."

"I wonder if fish are nonbinary?" I put a finger to my chin as I followed Tim to the tanks. "Should your next betta use they/them pronouns?"

"Well." Tim huffed. "No. Because I don't get to decide for my fish what his pronouns are."

"But how are we supposed to know what they are if he doesn't tell us?"

Tim stopped next to a tank filled with neon tetras. "We won't know. Not until it happens."

"Then how can you assume the fish uses he/him? Makes more sense to use they/them as every fish then."

"The pretty bettas are all assigned male at birth, m'kay?" My roomie spun on one white rubber sole. "Don't make me sound transphobic."

"I know you're not, Apple Johnnyseed." I shaded my eyes like Sam

Neill seeing the dinosaur in *Jurassic Park*. "If you want help, you can go back to Glenda over there."

Glenda stood in our line of sight, behind a checkout counter, arms folded across her apron.

"Excuse me?" Tim called. "Is there someone here to help?"

Glenda rolled her eyes and stalked across the store. "I already asked if you wanted help."

"Oh, I wasn't sure if there was someone who was a fish expert."

"And you didn't think I was a fish expert?"

Tim bit his lip. "No, no, I mean... I can't assume everyone is... you know..."

"My friend, you can't recover," I whispered in his ear as Glenda stared. "Give up now."

We let the awkward silence pass through. Then Tim chirped, "Can you tell us where the bettas are?"

As Tim pondered which betta to release from its plastic container prison, I focused on the tank of plecos in front of me.

The hardy, speckled gray creatures were small now, but they would expand to fit any tank they were placed in. I only knew this because my ex was hooked on aquarium videos (har har). She never actually built a tank, but she'd watch all sorts of niche YouTube celebrities construct them out of bathtubs, old televisions, even a vending machine. Plecos were never the subjects of the videos, but they cruised along in the background, quietly removing the algae from the environment.

Plecos were me. I was plecos. That was part of why Nicole and I broke up to begin with. She had to be the center of attention, and I was suffocating in her shadow. I couldn't afford rent by myself, so Tim pulled me into his charming orbit. Little did I know it would lead to even more aquatic obsession, albeit a different kind.

"Katy!" Tim snapped his fingers in front of my nose. "Focus. Which one?"

I couldn't see a lot of difference between them. They were different colors: blue, red, purple. There was a glowing one—I assumed it was made from the same technology that produced the neon tetras. I didn't want to know how they did that. I also didn't want a fish that could go nuclear at any time. I'd seen the *Simpsons* episode where the orange one sprouts three eyes.

"Um." I pointed to one with shimmering teal fins. "He's pretty."

Tim looked heavenward, as if apologizing for me. "He's the same color as Ringo was. That won't do."

"So." Once again, I perused the offerings. "Do any of these not resemble a betta you have owned before?"

Tim gave me side-eye.

"A betta who has... been your companion before?"

"That is the correct answer."

We faced the lines of what seemed like a hundred little homes. "How about this little guy?" I indicated a red betta with a streak of purple on his back. "He wants to go home with you."

The fish did look sad, although I was pretty sure bettas came installed with RBF. His tiny eyes were liquid, though, and they seemed to meet mine. *Come on,* the fish seemed to say. *Take me home.*

"Hmmm. He does resemble Rick Astley. But then again, Rick wasn't Ringo." Tim sighed, presumably at the memory. "Yes, he's a contender. Get him."

I reached for the container, then stopped. "Are there going to be... multiple contenders?"

"Why do you ask?"

"I can't carry a precarious pile of fish to the checkout. I'll drop them and Glenda will eat me."

Tim blew out a breath. "Okay. Let's take Bowie home."

"Wow. You like him that much, huh?" I lifted Bowie from the shelf and held him up so I could see in those eyes again.

Tim looked worried. "Is he not a Bowie? Should I go with Elton? Or Prince. We haven't had a Prince yet, and he is kind of purple..."

"No." I shook my head firmly. "He's a Bowie."

WE DECIDED to bum around a little. Thirtysomethings without interpersonal commitments didn't have much else to do on Friday nights. I got a cart, and Tim made sure the fish was safe in the top part meant for babies. Bowie needed reliable transportation.

We sauntered through rows of brightly colored birds, mostly smaller ones like parakeets and conures. A sturdy steel cage contained a few cats sponsored by the local humane society, and I peeked in to admire their sweet faces. Tim had to check in the fish supply section to make sure he had everything he needed for Bowie's new home.

Around the back of the store, near the bathrooms, there was a clearance table. "Oh," said Tim sadly. "It's the pets no one wanted!"

I scoffed. "It's probably just Christmas dog costumes and off-brand cat food."

"No, look." Tim pointed.

There was indeed a small creature on the end of the table, held in a large see-through tank filled with rodent bedding. It was hidden deep, so it was hard to tell. "Gerbils are the ones with the long tails, right?" I asked as I examined the tank.

"Yeah." Tim scratched his head. "Don't tell me you want to take that thing home. I thought you didn't like animals anyway."

I stuck out my tongue. "I just think your obsession with fish is strange."

Someone cleared their throat from behind us. Glenda stood there, magically transported from the front of the store, and I felt my neck go hot. Tim leaned against the cart, and it rattled, jostling Bowie. He immediately bent down and began whispering sweet nothings to the fish. I rolled my eyes.

"We're closed," Glenda said. She pointed to the ceiling. I hadn't noticed that half the lights were out.

"Oh." I turned away from the hamster. Was it making chittering noises inside the container? "Okay, we'll check out. But... how much is this little guy?"

Glenda smacked her lips. "Four bucks."

The lady smelled like sweat and cheap perfume. Her presence was oddly unnerving. I wanted to get out of there right away. But I didn't know if I should take the hamster or not. It would be a lot of work, but it might be worth it to have a friend, especially now that I was so alone.

Four dollars for a hamster? That seemed so cheap. "What's the catch?"

"He's not popular with the kiddos."

"Oh," Tim said. "Just get him! We can come back tomorrow if we need more supplies."

In a flash, Glenda stepped past me and picked up the tank. She deposited it inside the cart with a clang. Then she began hauling feed and bedding from the table beside it. When she started marching to the cash register, we followed her and didn't ask any questions.

EVERY TIME I pulled into our complex's parking lot, I said a prayer of thanks to the universe. Tim's parents paid for a spacious two-bedroom in a luxury development. The lobby smelled of new carpet and fresh paint. Inside, every fixture was stainless steel, and there were oodles of cabinets and closets. I didn't have much, so most of the storage was filled with Tim's brightly colored clothes and sparkly drag outfits. But my little room was my sanctuary, and I was grateful.

We took Bowie upstairs and got him situated in the tank that held so many ghosts of fish past. I also carried the rodent supplies and dumped them on our dining room table in preparation for hauling my hamster upstairs. It turned out that me carrying it was easier than trying to move it together, so Tim held doors open for me while I sweated it out.

I placed the hamster tank on the dining room table next to its items. Tim was already raising an eyebrow.

"What? I'm gonna move it as soon as I find a spot in my room."

"You live like a monk. There's plenty of space." Tim executed the look down his nose that always made me feel stupid. "How about on top of your dresser?"

"Yeah, I guess that's fine."

Tim tsked. "Don't get salty on me. I'll help you move it in there and then I'm going to bed. 'Kay?"

"Fine." I was bristling inside. A side effect of being grateful—I felt like I had to take his crap, which usually came out of nowhere. I should have known he'd get protective of the antique table he'd scored for a song at the vintage furniture store.

Once the rodent was safely installed on my dresser, Tim blew me a kiss and flounced into his room. Maybe he thought nothing of our minor spat, but I still felt stung.

I tapped on the glass and cooed. "You can come out! I want to see you."

No motion from inside. I glimpsed its brown fur through a heap of taupe bedding. I did have to feed and water him—luckily, the tank had come with a bowl and water dripper, which I assumed they'd used at the store. Poor thing, stuck on the clearance table. I knew how it felt to be discarded, tossed aside. I returned to the living room and poured kibble into its dish, then filled the dripper with new water.

Once I re-mounted the items, I waited for a few minutes to see if the hamster would come out. But all I saw was rustling inside. I changed into pajamas, brushed my teeth, read for a little while. And it never did come out. I tapped the glass again, and I could see it move, but it didn't approach the food or water. I went to bed nervous that he was on clearance because it was defective.

THAT NIGHT I woke to keening. It sounded like a baby, mournful yet edgy, and I could not fall back asleep while it continued. I even closed the window, but the sound persisted. I wasn't sure how long it kept going, but eventually it gave way to an operatic sort of singing. What kind of party were my neighbors throwing on a Sunday night?

My bakery call time was five a.m., so my general wake-up time was at about four. Whoever was practicing their arias kept me up until the alarm went off. When I got up, though, the music eerily stopped. I was grumpy as I got ready, but at least when I checked in the tank, my

rodent had consumed some of his food and water. He continued to
hide, but I at least knew he was alive.

If there was any plus to getting up so early, it was how quiet the
streets were in the morning. The night took on a different quality sometime around four. Pressing the snooze button on the sunrise. This was
the domain of crepuscular creatures, hunting in a lightening night.

The bakery was a stout brick building on the main drag of the
small, quaint town that bordered the larger one Tim and I lived in. This
town was so insular, inhabited by the wealthy, and even Tim with his
trust fund couldn't afford it. But it was a good place to work, at least
until recently. I'd been looking for another job ever since Nicole and I
split, putting hundreds of applications out there and praying to the
universe for a bite.

I parked behind the shop and entered through the back door.
Coffee was already brewing, the scent mixing with that of the pastry
dough. Nicole had her hands in a big lump of it, kneading and rolling.
"Hey, Katy," she said with an artificial smile.

"Morning." I slung my purse into a corner and headed for the bathroom to wash my hands. As I rinsed, my face in the mirror scowled
back at me.

She had carefully cultivated a new playlist, one that didn't include
any of "our songs." A lot of emo rock, but nothing too mournful. It
served its purpose—to keep us from having to work in awkward
silence.

Nicole is not a petty person. But she hadn't known how to break up
with me, especially considering she's the daughter of the bakery
owners, and she didn't want me to lose my job. We'd worked together
for six months, dated for another six, then lived together for a year and
a half. I had no idea that anything was wrong even as she slipped away
from me. Eventually I caught her with a guy—we're both bi—and
considering it wasn't my apartment, I had to leave.

It was too bad I still loved her.

I caught myself staying up too late writing mournful poems like a
seventh grader. Obsessing over losing her like she was my breath. (And
yes, writing overly purple prose like that.) Now, as I nursed my coffee

for a moment, I couldn't stop myself from watching her. She was always so intent on her work, whether it was starting new bakes or meticulously icing cookies. Her lips twisted, her dark pink hair wrangled into a ratty ponytail, covered in flour—none of that mattered. She was beautiful.

*Goddamnit, Katy.* I put my coffee down on the shiny metal table and got to work.

WE OPENED AT SEVEN, which gave me a break from being around Nicole. She stayed in the back while I ran the register. Our usuals were there first—office managers grabbing donuts for their teams, the local coffee shop owner picking up scones and bagels to sell. Once the rush passed, traffic was intermittent.

Tim arrived at eight, as he did before heading to his job. I always made a latte for myself and one for him around that time. I looked forward to his short visits—especially since the business with Nicole—but today his face was stormy.

"Your hamster." He approached the counter and snatched the latte from my hand.

"Okay, brat." I scowled. "What's wrong with it?"

"That's not the issue." Tim took a long swallow of the hot drink and if he burned his tongue, he didn't show it. He dug his phone out of a pocket and pulled up his photo app. "What the Sam Hill is this?"

I squinted at the screen. Our living room was trashed. Holes chewed into the couch, long ruts carved into the carpet, chairs knocked over and scratched.

"Shit." I shook my head and reached for my drink. I was going to need some major caffeine to get through this day, and probably alcohol later. "But there's no way that was my rodent. I haven't even seen it come out of its bedding."

"'What else could it be? I woke up and the house was like this." He rubbed his brow, and I saw the tension in his temples.

I didn't have any words. I hadn't even named my hamster. Hadn't

even seen his little face. And yet I felt defensive. This wasn't my fault...
right?

"I'm sorry, Tim." My body deflated. "Do you want a donut? I
promise to figure this out when I get home."

"No." He waved a hand. Didn't look at me. I noticed he wore a drab
gray shirt and a purple tie with a subtle geometric pattern. It wasn't his
style at all. "We'll talk later."

As he left, the little bell above the door tinkling, I felt a lump
growing in my throat. The store was empty for now save for a woman
reading her Kindle with the coffee I'd just served her. I turned on a heel
and went in the back just before the tears came.

Nicole was wiping her forehead with her arm. She caught my eye,
and her expression changed. "What's wrong?"

"Nothing." I blinked salt out of my eyes, the tears mixing with sweat
from the hot kitchen.

"It doesn't look like nothing."

I could not explain this to her, so I went with the simplest answer.
"Tim and I had a fight."

She nodded, looked down. I was certain she felt guilty, knowing I
lived with him because of her, but maybe not. Maybe she was just
embarrassed that I was having emotions in front of her and there was
nothing she could do about it.

"I'll cover the register," she said, brushing past me, and I caught the
scent of her vanilla and lemon shampoo.

I leaned against the wall and slid all the way down to the hard floor.
I knew my jeans would be dark with dirt when I got up, but it didn't
matter. I needed to be this close to the ground to indulge in my
sobbing.

WHEN I GOT HOME, I surveyed the damage.

It was worse in person. The carpet was practically gored. Tufts of
fabric from the couch littered the floor. Even the closet doors had been
knocked apart, my shoes chewed on.

Eventually the shock wore off, and panic shot through me. A hamster could not be capable of this, and yet what else could it be? The creature was the only new factor in our household since the night before. *Tim's* household. I'd be kicked out for certain, and I'd still have to pay for everything to be fixed, and my bank account had exactly $48.53 in it. If I hadn't have bought the damn hamster, it would have been more.

I stomped into my room and pulled off the lid of the tank. Perhaps against my better judgment, I dug my hands into the bedding, shredding it. "Where are you, you motherfucker?" I yelled. "You haven't even been here twenty-four hours."

But there was nothing in there. No frantic heart beating, no warm furry rodent pushing itself into a corner away from my hands.

Tears kept streaming down my face. I stomped the floor hard and screamed at the top of my lungs.

Then I tore everything apart—everything that hadn't already been destroyed. I opened all the kitchen cabinets and took the pots and pans out. I moved the couch from against the wall. I opened the closet and threw shoes and clothes out behind me, Tim's size-eleven heels, my winter coat. I picked up every piece of furniture, opened every vent, reached behind every bookshelf until my dry hands scraped and bled.

When I couldn't search any longer, I flopped out onto the ripped carpet. I couldn't cry anymore either, so I fell asleep.

"Dear God. This looks worse than before."

I raised my head to see Tim looking down at me with a disgusted expression.

I'd drooled all over my face. My back was stiff, cracking, my feet reaching out for purchase so I could get up. "'M sorry," I said, sleep rasping my voice. "I was trying to find it."

"You didn't even find it?" He boggled at me.

I made my way up to my feet, but he was so much taller than me that I still felt like a child being punished. "I did my best."

"Katy. Really. I've got a show tonight." Tim dropped his satchel and glared. "I don't need this."

"You don't have to say it. I get it." I rubbed my eyes. "And I'll pay for all of it. Somehow."

"I'm not sure if you can. You can check with the leasing office, but they might charge us extra rent or something."

"I'll do it. I swear. I'll get the thing out of here too."

"Katy." Tim's frown softened. He came closer to me, put a hand on my shoulder. "You didn't know."

"But I can fix it." I sniffled. "I'll stay home tonight. I don't want to leave it alone in the house."

For a second, I thought Tim would say no, of course I should come to the show. I thought he would say that I was making too much of an issue out of the hamster and that everything would be fine. I thought he might hug me.

He clapped his hand on my shoulder and nodded. "I think that's best."

I SNUCK out when Tim was getting ready and drove my rattletrap Corolla to PetSmart.

The moment I walked in, my gaze fixated immediately on Glenda. She stood on a ladder in the fish section, swirling an orange net in one of the tanks.

I marched toward her, hands on hips, practically baring my teeth. "What did you sell me?"

Glenda turned, impassive. "Whadya mean?"

"That thing on the clearance rack."

"You mean the hamster?"

"Whatever the fuck it is."

"Hey now." Glenda licked her lips, creepily, like a snake. "We don't swear in here. Or we get kicked out."

"They should kick you out for letting me buy that. Not a hamster. It destroyed my living room." I grabbed my phone and swiped through my photos, thrusting it up at her when I found the right one. "What does that? Did you, like, curse it or something?"

Glenda stared.

"I need to return it." My hands were shaking. "I can't have this thing anymore."

No reaction.

"Please. My roommate is going to kick me out." I put my hands together, begging. Fish swam peacefully beside me as if nothing was wrong. "Take it back."

"No returns on clearance items," Glenda said sharply.

She turned back to the tank. Her net snared a fat goldfish. She pulled it out and dumped it into a plastic bag.

"I need to speak to your manager. This is ridiculous." I ground my teeth against the words.

Glenda moved slowly down the ladder until she could step down from it. She turned to face me. "I am the manager."

"Corporate, then. There must be some kind of insurance." I brightened—I hadn't thought of the possibility. "If something I get here damages my home, it has to be covered."

"Not on clearance items." Glenda pushed past me and walked up to a PA microphone. "Nolan family, your fish is ready."

I stood dumbfounded as a young white child with golden hair and a missing tooth approached. She took the fish bag from Glenda's hand and grinned. Her two moms rolled up behind her and grinned too. There was so much joy in that moment.

Glenda turned back to me. "Anything else I can do for you?"

I watched the family push their cart to the register, armed with their fish and sheer bliss, and shook my head.

TIM REALLY WAS gorgeous as Apple Johnnyseed. His wig was long and blonde, real corn-fed hair that must have cost a fortune. He wore a plaid shirt with denim overalls and carried a pitchfork. And his makeup was perfection: light shadow under the brow shading down to a darker shade against his long lashes.

When he came home, I was in the kitchen making ramen on the stove. He passed me at first, without saying anything, but then paused at the door. I caught his eye through the window between the kitchen and living room. "Yes?"

"Take it easy," he said, pursing his glossy lips.

The door slammed. I was alone with my thoughts and with a reckless menace.

Before Tim left, I'd put all the furniture back where it was and cleaned up as much as I could. All that was left of the carnage was the streaks in the couch and carpet. Carpet couldn't be that expensive to replace, and I could go to the furniture store and get a new couch with one of those zero percent interest financing deals. Tim could pick it out. It was a good reason to freshen up the apartment.

After finishing my ramen, I pulled up my Nicole playlist on my phone and grabbed my laptop. Scrolled through apartment listings. Someone on craigslist had a place down by the bakery, an open room, but the photos reminded me too much of our old apartment. They were probably in the same building. Talk about awkward, especially if I ran into her boyfriend. "Hey, man," I'd say. "Been a while since I saw you naked with my ex, huh?"

My stomach roiled. I'd have to move back in with my parents. I'd have to borrow the money to fix Tim's apartment and then go crawling back into their basement like a troll. "All By Myself" would be playing on the background soundtrack in my head as I hefted boxes down the stairs. Maybe I'd even fall and hit the ground with a twisted ankle.

Quitting the bakery would be good though.

I texted my mom, but she didn't answer.

Before long I was doomscrolling through the various social media voids. My eyes were drooping when I felt a warm, furry body at my side.

My heart picked up.

This was not a rodent at all. It looked like a rabbit. How had it shoved itself so deeply into that tank? And somehow it had hid the gigantic antlers that sprouted from its forehead.

Ah. That would explain the goring.

The animal sniffed my hand and curled up close beside me like a cat. I goggled at it and prayed it wouldn't gouge my skin or clothes.

"Do you know that you just ruined my life?" I asked it.

It looked up at me and twitched its nose.

"If you expect me to keep you around, you'll have to shape up."

It did not answer.

With the creature still nestled beside me, I picked up my phone and searched for "rabbit with horns."

Images came back immediately: page after page of results for something called a jackalope. I squinted at the screen, rolling through the articles. Jackalopes were sometimes vicious, sometimes docile, and prone to mischief. They could sing and mimic human voices. Some legends said they manifested good luck. "Not you," I said with a snort, and the jackalope twitched its nose.

Maybe I could let it go. It could live in the bushes outside our complex, and I could go out there and feed it. If Tim would let me stay. If I had to move, I could bring it with me. I'd only have to make it behave until I found someplace to live.

I shook my head at nothing. I was kidding myself. This thing didn't have loyalty to me. It only had itself to look out for. It had only been a minute since I even saw it. How could I feel so connected to it now?

I needed to go to bed.

I gently separated the creature from my side.

It let out a squeak, and then a roar.

Like nothing I've ever heard. A primeval kind of scream, high-pitched and inhuman. It leaped off my lap and hopped down the hall, moving faster than any rabbit I'd ever seen.

It was heading for Tim's room.

"No!" I shouted and sprinted after it. It had already disappeared, was somewhere among Tim's discarded outfits and makeup palettes.

And Bowie. *Oh, shit.*

I careened into the room and crouched next to the fish tank. Bowie swam peacefully, tracing languid circles in the water. I let out a long breath. I had to stay here and make sure the jackalope didn't jump onto the tank stand. I couldn't fall asleep. Had to stay vigilant.

"Oh. My. God."

Tim stood in the doorway. I had fallen asleep. My phone was in the living room, and I had no idea what time it was. I startled and cast my eyes up to the tank. Thank God it was still right side up.

"He's fine," I mumbled, blinking, getting to my feet. I kept falling asleep in odd places. It was too bad I didn't have money for a chiropractor. "I came in here to make sure he would be okay."

"Why?" Tim pulled his wig off and threw it. It landed on the pink carpet and pooled into a lump vaguely resembling a creature. "Is your pet in here?"

He practically spat the words. I couldn't believe that just a day ago we'd been tromping through the PetSmart like best buds. The jackalope had destroyed us in a matter of hours.

I cringed. "I don't know."

"Katy, I can't have this." He sat down on the bed and slumped. "I'm getting texts from the neighbors about how loud it is up here."

I remembered my stomping and screaming. My cheeks flushed.

"Look, Nicole was at the show tonight."

I bristled. "And?"

"She wasn't with anyone."

"I don't care."

Tim scratched the top of his head. His lipstick and gloss had worn off, and now he looked like a kid who had gotten into his mom's makeup drawer. "She offered to take you in for a while until you can find a place."

Even though I knew it was coming, I didn't believe he'd kick me out so soon. How could I be so stupid?

"I'm gonna take a shower and spend the night at Jackson's." He got up and started digging in his drawers for clothes. "Nic is going to close the bakery tomorrow so she can help you move."

THAT NIGHT, alone, I heard the crying again.

I tossed and turned, nervous about the morning, whatever time she planned to get here. What I would say to her. How I would get the jackalope into its tank, at least long enough to let it go into the woods.

"I know, I know, you're sad!" I yelled. "So am I! Now shut up and let me sleep!"

After a few more pitiful moans, the jackalope followed my orders.

The brisk knock came at six. It wasn't too early—Nicole and I were both used to the morning hours—but I didn't feel ready. I hadn't showered, my stuff wasn't packed, and I didn't know where the jackalope was.

Normally she would have come in unannounced, key jingling in the lock. We were together so often that it would only be when she returned from errands or trips to the warehouse store for bulk supplies. The alone time was nice, I can't lie about that, but whenever I heard her come in I'd jump up and meet her at the door. Like I did now.

Her hair was up in its usual ponytail, her face scrubbed clean. Even with no makeup, her lashes were so long, skin unblemished. "Are you ready?"

"I haven't packed." When I cast my eyes down to the carpet, I saw the streaks of jackalope horn carved into the pile. "But I don't have much. It won't take long. He only told me a few hours ago anyway."

Nicole nodded. I felt her gaze fall to the floor too. "I get it. It's okay."

I filled suitcases and the few boxes I had from moving away in the first place. I shoved toiletries in my duffel bag. Carried my bedspread and laptop directly to the car. Nicole's RAV-4 wasn't huge, but it had enough trunk space to fit most of my things, especially after we folded down the rear seats. But I hadn't grabbed the final item.

"The fucking jackalope," I muttered.

When I turned to Nicole, her eyes were narrowed. "The what now?"

I pulled out my phone and showed her the articles I had found. "I accidentally adopted this," I told her. "It was on clearance at the pet store."

Her lip twisted. "Are you kidding?"

I shook my head somberly. She glanced at me, then back at the phone, then back at me again. Then she burst out laughing.

I bristled. "It's not funny!"

I left her standing by the car as I went back up to the apartment. Checked inside the tank. It wasn't there, not that I thought it would be. I hefted it to the center of the living room, hoping that if I could catch the thing, I could put it right into the tank and be done with it. The question was how to lure it out.

Sitting on the couch had worked before. I sat and blinked, viewing my surroundings. The shameful cuts in the carpet. "Where are you?" I called, making some halfhearted pursed-lips noises. No response.

The stomps of Nic's Doc Martens came up the stairs. She came in and lingered in the doorway. "Any luck?"

"I'm gonna Google." The page of info on the jackalope was still pulled up in a tab on my phone. I skimmed it quickly but didn't find anything about luring one out, so I kept looking. There were pages and pages of articles. My eyelids were drooping. Once we got to Nicole's and unpacked, I'd hit the couch.

Nicole reached inside her hoodie for her phone. She started typing too. God. She always had to find the answer first. She always had to one-up me somehow.

Never mind, it didn't matter, it was over. I scrolled faster.

"Whiskey," Nicole drawled. "Have you tried that?" She turned the screen so I could see the page she'd found.

My insides boiled. "They like whiskey?"

"Yeah, it's on the cryptid wiki." She tossed her hair and smirked. "You have any?"

"Tim might." I got up and checked the liquor cabinet. There was a handle of Jim Beam, and I poured a tiny bit into a cereal bowl. I set it on the floor.

"Are you supposed to call it or something?" Nicole asked.

"I don't know. Maybe you should look it up," I said on the edge of my teeth.

"Whoa, whoa. Calm down, tiger." But she glanced down at her phone anyway. "Hope it doesn't take long."

"Ah, yes, because I'm inconveniencing you." I stared at the amber liquid rotating gently in the bowl. I couldn't look at her. She didn't respond to that one.

We stood for a few minutes before the jackalope emerged. It stuck its pink nose out from behind the couch, sniffing the air, then hopped toward the bowl. Behind me, I heard Nicole's phone hit the ground with a thump.

The jackalope nonchalantly lapped the whiskey, letting its sharp scent into the air. I crouched beside it, getting ready to pick it up.

"It's real," Nicole breathed.

My limbs jangled with anger. This was why we didn't work. Because she treated me like I was stupid. She didn't even have the decency to break up with me before she moved on.

I shot back up and turned. "Are you still dating him?"

Nicole blinked. "What?"

"That guy."

She bent over to get her phone. Whatever awe that had been in her expression slid off her face. "We've got more important problems right now."

The jackalope hadn't moved. It seemed content. I took a step forward.

"If I'm going to stay at your house, I need to know."

Nicole rolled her eyes. "No one lives there except me."

"But I might see him." I clenched my fists. "Won't that be awkward?"

"Not if you don't make it awkward. Did you think you'd be sleeping in my bed?"

I wanted to punch her in that button nose, pull that bandanna off her pigtailed head, stomp on her cute toes. Shred her Birkenstocks. The jackalope could help me with that. I needed to give it a name. Jackalope, Destroyer of Worlds. Jackalope, Siege of the Land.

No matter what I did, I wasn't going to dignify that last comment with an answer.

I crouched down again and approached carefully until I was toe to toe with the jackalope. I looped my arms around it from the bottom. It didn't struggle. I lifted it into the tank and adjusted the bedding around it, tucking it in. "Let's go," I said to Nicole, not meeting her eyes.

"Seems you're the jackalope whisperer," she said.

*Better than being an asshole,* I thought.

AT LEAST SHE helped me get my stuff into the apartment.

The tank was the last thing to come inside. We put it on the balcony. I planned to release my jackalope that night.

I pulled up a wicker chair from the patio set. We'd spent so many nights here, smoking pot or drinking wine or both. Having long, deep conversations. I had been attracted to her intellect and often thought she was wasting it on the bakery.

The jackalope and I sat in comfortable silence as the breeze played over us. It stayed buried in its bedding. I sneaked into Nicole's fridge and ripped a few slices from a head of lettuce. One advantage of her holier-than-thou vegan diet. I slipped the leaves into the tank and smiled as the jackalope came out to munch on them.

Eventually my head dipped back to my phone. I hadn't checked my email since this whole ordeal started. I pulled up a playlist on Spotify and reluctantly dived in.

Of course my inbox was an avalanche of auto-rejections from the jobs I'd been applying to. I wanted that sous-chef position at a fancy restaurant—it'd be a better opportunity to use my culinary degree. But I'd put my name in for desk jobs, manual labor, hospital transporters. Anything I was qualified for.

Then I heard a harmony I'd never noticed under one of the old Evanescence tracks I liked to listen to. A remix? I had the free version of Spotify, so the app was probably suggesting a song I didn't actually pick. I listened more closely, trying to pick out the alto notes under the melody.

By the time the final chorus started, I had located the source of the sound. The jackalope crooned beside me, its jaw barely open, laying down that pleasing harmonic thread.

I stared at it. "You need a name."

It continued singing, now humming along to an old-school Tori Amos track.

"How am I supposed to know what gender you are? You won't let me check your rear, I assume."

*Well, does it matter?*

"Okay, your pronouns will be they/them unless you inform me otherwise. As for a name..." I put a finger to my chin. "Kali, I think."

The Hindu goddess of destruction.

LATER THAT NIGHT, I took Kali downstairs and knelt in the grass behind the building. It wasn't dark yet, but the streetlights had already come on.

I placed them on the ground. "You're free now."

Kali wrinkled their nose and wiggled their horns.

"I know you don't want to go. But you can't stay in Nic's house." I sighed. "I'll be here, at least for a little bit. There is that empty apartment, too."

Kali only stared.

"I promise I'll be here! I'll bring you leaves. None of that gross old hamster food anymore. And look at all that foliage." I spread my hands. "You'll be so much happier here."

No movement from Kali. I got up, swallowing my tears. "I have to go."

I turned to head back up to the building. I needed to clean out the tank and put it on the curb. Then go sit glassy-eyed on the couch until I fell asleep. Until I had to go to my job with my ex-girlfriend, like we used to when things were good.

At the back door, I turned to make sure Kali had disappeared into the woods.

They had not. They were sitting right next to my ankle. I almost tripped. "Fuck!" I yelled, possibly disturbing the neighbors but not really caring. "What are you doing?!"

Kali growled, low in their throat.

"You can't blame me for leaving. I can't keep you in the apartment! But I'll stay here, okay? I'll make sure you are okay."

Another growl—but this time it was across the lawn.

A creature slunk behind the trees. Some kind of big animal. The snarl came again, bigger this time, and I saw it come forward.

It was a fucking bear.

"Shit, Kali. I can't let it get you." I leaned down to scoop them up, my heart speeding.

But Kali hopped away from me. They were moving toward the bear.

I inched backwards. All I could do was watch. I could have run, but I'd promised Kali I would make sure they were okay.

The bear roared. Kali leapt for it. My heart melted—they'd be crushed. A fitting end to these two horrible days. I couldn't watch. They deserved better than that.

I heard them both cry out again as I buried my face in my hands and squeezed my eyes tight. I was rooted to the spot. My first plan was to get away from the bear. Later, I'd come back and search for the remnants of Kali. Find a quiet space to bury them.

Then there was a massive thud. My eyes flew open.

Kali was hopping from the bear back to me. It was stone dead, lying flat on the ground, eyes staring up at nothing. Steaming intestines spilled from its abdomen. Kali had gored it top to bottom.

I CARRIED KALI BACK INSIDE. Nic was lying on the couch eating pizza rolls and messing around on her phone. She raised her head as we jostled through the door. "Whoa. What happened to you?"

We were covered in blood. The coppery smell of which did not blend well with the scent of fake Italian spices.

"Oh, no big deal. Kali just killed a bear in your backyard. What's good on TikTok these days?"

Nic dropped her phone. "What?"

I waved vaguely toward the back of the apartment. "Bear. Dead. Gotta call animal control. But I don't think they're in the office this late."

"You gotta be fucking kidding me." Nicole got up and headed for her Uggs. "I need to see this."

While she was outside, I grabbed some junk ads from the dining room table and spread them on the ground. Kali's fur was matted with the goopy liquid and possibly some entrail remnants. I gagged as I placed the creature on the paper.

"Do you want me to wash you?" I asked. At this point, I wouldn't have been surprised if they answered me.

The jackalope just looked at me with liquid eyes.

"Okay, message received. How about I put you in the tank?"

No response, but they also didn't seem fazed by the idea, so I took it as fine.

I was hauling the tank back in from the porch when Nicole banged through the door, her chest heaving.

"Pretty cool, huh?" I raised an eyebrow at her as I picked Kali up and put them in the tank surrounded by their bedding and the bloody newspapers.

Nicole flopped back onto the couch, still breathing heavily, and pulled her phone out of her hoodie pocket. She patted the seat next to her. I ignored her and went to the fridge to get Kali's vegetables.

"C'mon, Katy. You gotta see these pictures. This is insane."

"Well, I did see the whole thing happen." I placed half a head of lettuce and a fat carrot into Kali's tank. They went nuts for it. Bear-killing must have made the jackalope hungry. "Like I said, I'll call animal control in the morning. Should we call the landlord?"

"Yeah, if he doesn't hear before that." Nicole shuddered as she swiped across her screen. "I think I need a drink. You want a glass of wine?"

I took a deep breath and didn't sit next to her. I chose the armchair across from the couch. She'd discarded her Uggs. Her socks were white with tiny skulls screenprinted on them.

When we were together, I'd never noticed all these little details. Her cheeks were flushed by the cold, the tops of her ears red.

If I accepted the wine, I might sleep with her. If we fell back into our old ways, at least. But if she rejected me, that would hurt just as badly, and I didn't want either situation. Best to keep my inhibitions to myself. "No, that's fine," I said.

Nicole didn't move. She glanced at Kali, who continued to nibble their carrot. "I don't know what to think of all this."

Did she think I knew?

"I mean, not..." she went on. "You. Here. Us."

Oh, no. We were not going down this road. I kept my mouth shut. She could fall all over her words. I was done emotionally destroying myself.

"I feel bad. I didn't realize how much I hurt you."

I shrugged. "It's not like I had a choice."

She leaned forward over the coffee table. "It isn't fair. I'm the one who messed up. I should have let you stay here, at least until you found a place."

"But I did find a place." *And I lost it.*

"A place of your own. Where you're not bound to someone else because they're paying for it."

Blood rushed into my cheeks. "What else am I going to do? Ask your dad to give me a raise?"

"No, I mean..." Nic didn't seem to know what to do with her hands. She kept waving them like she was trying to create her thoughts out of the air. "You deserve so much more than me."

Yesterday I would have said no. Yesterday I would have begged her to take me back. But today was a different day. And neither one of us talked for a long time after that.

THERE WAS no moaning or keening that night. Kali sang a lullaby before I fell asleep, and then she was quiet.

I WOKE up and stared at the ceiling.

Nicole was gone. She must have left for the bakery without me. It was fine. I didn't want to go in anyway, and it was already daylight, so I'd be late. Plus I had to call someone about the bear.

Kali had buried themself in the bedding again. I was glad they were sleeping peacefully.

My phone was on the floor beside the couch. I leaned over and snatched it, yawning as I opened my email box. So many unread messages. Junk, promo, coupon, listservs...

Then a new address in the *from* column. *Hiring@roastandrutabaga.com*

Roast and Rutabaga. I'd heard of that, but I couldn't remember where. Was it a restaurant? I tapped on the email.

*Hello, Kathryn!* My government name. *We received your application and would love to talk to you about the sous-chef position we have open. When can you meet?*

I sat up straight and set to respond, my fingers flying. I didn't even have to think about it. *Anytime! I'm so looking forward to meeting you!*

When I finished the message, heart caught in my throat, I turned to see Kali's pink nose sticking out of the bedding.

SATURDAY CAME, and with it another drag show. Nicole was going with her boyfriend. Even though he wasn't the same guy she'd cheated on me with, I really did not want to be the third wheel. But I needed to talk to Tim. He wasn't answering my texts, and I needed to clear the air.

The ride to the bar wasn't as awkward as I thought it would be.

Elijah was a lovely man, and Nicole had lost her shine. I'd always ache for what we had, but after the past few days, I'd remembered why we weren't compatible. Watching her was bittersweet, her pink hair gleaming under every lamppost we passed beneath.

I had hope, though. That I would move on from her couch. The team from Roast and Rutabaga planned to meet with me on Monday—the head chef, the HR rep, and the house manager. They were a new operation but were spun off from several other successful restaurants in the area. This one aimed to provide more affordable food without sacrificing quality. It sounded like an amazing opportunity.

And I hoped Tim would be happy for me. He might not understand, but I wanted to repair our friendship.

The venue was dark. Subtle hanging lights illuminated the full bar and the sides of the room. I thought I would get a contact high from the reek of pot. A few attendants dragged chairs out from a closet in the back, but a few people were dancing in the space that was left over. The vibe was fun, and the room buzzed with anticipation. Elijah and Nicole split off, and I sat alone on a stool.

"You drinking tonight?" The bartender sidled up. They were short, buzzed hair, red lipstick. Tattoos winding around their arms.

"Nah. Here for the show."

"Let me get you a Sprite, then? On the house?"

I peered at the person. "How did you know I liked Sprite?"

They winked. "I've seen you around."

THE SHOW WAS delightful as always. The queens came out afterward to meet and greet with the guests. Apple Johnnyseed stood by the stage, her makeup thick and contoured, face alight with a grin. She'd gone with a dress today, crushed purple velvet and body-hugging, but she accented it with a country-straw hat. She loved performing, and I loved seeing her do it.

I wedged my way into the line. The queens were local legends, and everyone wanted to see them after shows.

As the person in front of me stepped away, Tim raised his eyes to me, and the smile slid off his face.

I reached my hands out for his. Reluctantly, he put his into mine.

"I am so sorry." I mustered as much earnestness as I could. "My choices hurt you. Even though I didn't mean for Kali to do all of that. I didn't have to be so cavalier about it. Having a pet is a big deal."

He didn't say anything right away. His lips twitched, and his real-hair wig swayed gently on his shoulders.

"I don't get it," he finally said. "How a hamster could do all that." He bit his lip. "I felt bad because I blamed you for it. But later I started thinking there was no way. Someone must have broken in and ransacked the place."

"No, it was Kali." I squeezed his hands. "You won't believe it until you see them. But they're a jackalope."

"The fuck is a jackalope?"

"I'll show you later. But don't worry about me. I have a job interview next week."

Tim's hands flew to his mouth. "Oh my God! That's so awesome. You thinking about getting your own place?"

I nodded. "I can stay with Nic until I get my feet under me. I'm so thankful for everything you've done."

He reached in for a hug. We held each other for a long time. He smelled like his Old Spice shower gel with a heavy dash of perfume. It felt like coming home.

"Let's get a drink." Tim slung his arm around my shoulders. "It's not too weird with her, huh?"

I smiled. "I think I have it figured out."

**A few weeks later**

Tim called and left me a crying voicemail. "Bowie dieeeeeed," he moaned.

I texted him and set up a time to go to the pet store. I needed some stuff for Kali anyway.

My new job had started, which was great because I didn't have to see Nicole 24/7. We had become more like ships passing in the night. I worked in the evening now, so I usually had the apartment to myself when I was home.

I was going to stay with her for a little longer to ensure I had enough money for a security deposit and first and last month's rent. Roast and Rutabaga wasn't loaded, but they were paying me enough for me to find my own place, even if it was a studio apartment. I was okay with that. In fact, I felt untethered. Like I could move on now, even leave this city once I had some experience under my belt.

Tim and I met in the parking lot. I had Kali in their carrier, and I held it up. "You finally get to meet them."

He peeked in through the bars. Kali stared demurely out.

"This thing destroyed my apartment?" Tim tilted his head. "Wait. Are those horns?"

I patted the top of the carrier. "They were scared, but now they know me. And they protect me."

We got a cart and put Kali into the top where a child would normally ride. Back in the fish section, Glenda was restocking mollies. She turned to see us, recognized us. Her thick red eyebrows went up to her hairline, then relaxed.

Tim sauntered over to the rack of bettas in plastic tubs. Kali's nose stuck out of the carrier's slats.

Glenda met my eyes and smirked.

I smirked right back, turned the cart, and headed to the back of the store.

# LOVELAND FROG AND LOVELAND TOAD ARE FRIENDS

Loveland Frog crawled up out of his swamp and yawned. The sun was up, and the sky was clear. The damp smells of grass and muck renewed him. It would be a beautiful day. Loveland Frog was ready for whatever came his way.

A disembodied voice came from the rushes. "What do you say, Loveland Frog?"

Loveland Frog jumped. He landed back in the water with a splash. "Who's there?"

Loveland Toad hopped onto the shore. He was looking good today. His monstrous warts shone in the morning light. As Loveland Frog appraised him, he couldn't help smiling.

"How was your sleep?" Loveland Toad asked, heading toward him. Loveland Frog left his swamp to meet his friend halfway. They hugged. Loveland Frog stretched out his big arms and patted his webbed hands along Loveland Toad's back.

"Refreshing," said Loveland Frog. "And yours?"

"Excellent." Loveland Toad shaded his eyes with his leg. "What adventures shall we get into today?"

They hopped along the shore. Loveland Frog felt bad for all the regular frogs who couldn't keep up. Loveland Frog and Loveland Toad passed the swamp easily and headed to dry land. "There is my tree," Loveland Toad said, pointing as they went by.

"I know, I know," Loveland Frog said. "You tell me every time."

"And there's the house where we got big," Loveland Toad said, pointing to a structure in the distance.

Loveland Frog groaned. "You tell me that every time too."

The trees were turning red and gold. Loveland Frog searched them in concern. "It is almost time for us to hibernate," he said to his friend. "This is the first time we will hibernate since we became big."

Loveland Toad found a tree. He settled underneath it. The breeze was chilly in the shade. Loveland Frog settled beside his friend. He could feel the warmth between them.

"I can tell you are worried," said Loveland Toad. "I can always tell that about you."

"Because we are good friends," said Loveland Frog. He hiccupped out a ribbiting sound. Soon they would have to return to the pond for breakfast and a morning bath. He wished they could spend more time walking in the fields.

"Do you think hibernating will be different this year?" questioned Loveland Toad.

Loveland Frog sighed. "I do not know. I have never been big before."

Loveland Frog and Loveland Toad had always been adventurers. Even when they were small, they left the swamp for different pastures. One day this past spring, they'd ventured across the cornfields. Loveland Frog was very upset when they could not find water or food. Night fell, and Loveland Frog thought they would die in the cold. But they huddled together, like they did now, and they made it through the night. The next morning, they found the house. A hose dripped water onto pavement, and Loveland Frog hopped right into it, relishing the water on his skin. He could breathe again.

The question was then how they would get back. But a very large creature scooped them into its very large hands. Its skin was smooth and tasted like salt. Loveland Frog cried out as Loveland Toad was separated from him. Loveland Frog was dumped into a jar of chunky red liquid. It was not water, but at least he could breathe. Eventually, he fell asleep.

When he woke, he could not tell if it was night or day. He had never been in a place with no sun. Without the sun, they would not be able to get back at all. Loveland Frog was about to cry when he saw a huge creature cowering in the shadows.

"Loveland Toad, is that you?" he gasped.

Loveland Toad hiccupped and came forward. It was him, all right. He was huge. His webbed feet had grown huge and he stood on two of them. The other two sprouted out of his chest. Loveland Frog realized that if he could look Loveland Toad in the eye, that he was also big. Too big.

He was awkward as he lumbered toward Loveland Toad. They did not know what to do. Eventually, Loveland Frog patted Loveland Toad on the back with his new appendage. They would come to learn that these were called arms. They would come to learn about the naked-skinned animal that put them into the red liquid. But that was for another day.

Loveland Frog shook his head. He had been daydreaming. Loveland Toad still looked at him. Neither of them could decide whether hibernating would be different.

They went back. By the time they arrived at the swamp, the sun had moved high up into the sky. It baked the ground. Loveland Toad hovered at the edge of the water, waiting for a fat dragonfly or a chickadee. Loveland Frog preferred fish himself. He dived far below and swallowed a nice bass.

"Should we take a nap?" Loveland Toad suggested after they were both full.

Loveland Frog did often become tired after eating. He agreed.

Loveland Toad followed Loveland Frog into his home inside the swamp. Loveland Frog's hole was covered by a large outcropping of rock, where Loveland Toad could curl comfortably. Loveland Frog sank into the muck, and they enjoyed a long afternoon sleep.

It was nearly sundown when they woke and swam up out of the swamp. Loveland Frog loved this time of day, when the land around

them was soaked in burnished-gold sunlight. Loveland Toad appreci-
ated it too.

They only went to the woods behind the pond this time. Loveland
Toad was peckish, but Loveland Frog was still full from the bass. Loveland Toad found a few bumblebees. "I'm not in the mood for a chip-
munk," he said.

"See. You are full too," Loveland Frog said. He poked Loveland
Toad's warty shoulder.

"I am not," protested Loveland Toad. "You ate too much at
lunchtime."

They squabbled. Loveland Frog wanted to go back home, but Loveland Toad wanted to stay out. "Loveland Toad, I am tired," said Loveland Frog. "We should rest."

"We cannot rest." Loveland Toad stamped a big webbed foot. "We
do not know what is going to happen when we need to hibernate."

"But that is precisely why we need to rest." Loveland Frog yawned.
"We are getting more and more tired. Soon the snow will come, and we
will be too cold to survive."

Loveland Toad stopped and looked at him. "What is snow?"

Loveland Frog thought about the single time he had seen snow. He
had been just a little frog, curled up with his brothers and sisters in the
muck. When they woke up one morning, their mother was gone. Loveland Frog's brothers and sisters could not rouse themselves, but Loveland Frog could not go back to sleep. The water was freezing.

His mother could be up there. He could risk it for only a moment.
He swam up, dodging pieces of ice and frozen plants.

When he stuck his head out of the water, he saw nothing but white.
The shore, the water, all covered with this blinding white. Even if his
mother was there, he would not be able to find her. He could see
nothing but the tiny particles falling from the sky, made of ice but
turning into this white when it fell.

It was puzzling and troubling. Loveland Frog could do nothing
except turn back around and swim as fast as he could back into the
warmth of the muck. His brothers and sisters were all still there,
snoring away. He tucked himself back in among them, but he couldn't

tell how long it was before he finally fell asleep. He kept picturing that world up there, something he'd never seen, and how wild it was, and how terrible and beautiful.

Now, Loveland Frog cleared his throat. "Snow is frozen rain. It is best that we stay away from it."

Loveland Toad cocked his head as if he were thinking deeply about the concept. "Fascinating," he said.

Unfortunately, their squabbling had taken them onto a wrong path. Loveland Frog and Loveland Toad were shaking as the night grew colder. "We should not have gone this far," Loveland Frog said. "We need to find a warm place to rest."

Loveland Toad hung his head. "I am sorry, Loveland Frog. I did not realize we would get lost."

"We are lost," Loveland Frog said sadly.

"I hope this is not like what happened when we got big," Loveland Toad said.

"It is not." Loveland Frog did not want to be angry at his best friend. He wished he had convinced Loveland Toad to stay back at the pond. But it was too late now. The night had settled in. Loveland Frog could only smell dead leaves and muck, and the muck was not the kind from his home.

Then Loveland Toad pointed. "Look!"

There were lights up ahead. Loveland Frog lifted his neck to see. The lights went by for a long time and then suddenly disappeared. "What do you suppose that means?" Loveland Frog asked.

"I do not know. But maybe there is heat where there are lights."

Despite the cold, they moved more quickly, hopping along on their large, muscular legs. The lights streaked by faster and faster.

They came to a stop at a steep hill. When he was small, Loveland Frog could have climbed that hill with ease. Now his body was unruly and hard to control. Loveland Toad must have felt the same, because he did not move. "I am sorry I got us lost," he said.

"It is okay," Loveland Frog said. He felt bad for Loveland Toad. He should not have gotten so angry before.

"There is a path over here." It was hard to see, but there was a worn patch of grass beside the hill. Both Loveland Frog and Loveland Toad were able to hop up the hill.

But when they arrived, they were even more perplexed. They were beside a road, but not the dirt roads they were used to. This road stretched far beyond what they could see in the distance. It was covered in a strange substance. Loveland Toad picked his webbed foot up and inspected its bottom. "This is dust," he said. "It is curious."

"Very curious," agreed Loveland Frog. This was not the kind of dust that lay on the forest floor. It was gritty and black.

"There are the lights," said Loveland Toad.

"And they come with noises!" Loveland Frog yelled.

The noise was bigger than any noise Loveland Frog had ever heard. It rumbled against the ground and shook the earth below them. Loveland Frog was certain he would die when the noise reached him. He reached for Loveland Toad. "I love you, my friend!" he said.

"I can't hear you," yelled Loveland Toad.

But then the light blinded them. And then it was gone. Just like that, the silence returned.

"Maybe our blood will heat up now," Loveland Toad said. "Now that we are scared."

Loveland Frog was unhappy. He did not like being so far away from home. He did not like being afraid. Maybe adventuring was not for him after all. It always ended in sorrow. "We should go back," Loveland Frog said.

"I guess you are right," Loveland Toad said. "It will be easier to get back to where we came from than to venture further."

"We can hop faster than other creatures," Loveland Frog pointed out. "If we hurry, we can get back to the swamp before we get too cold."

They were about to leave the strange, scary place when there was another sound they did not recognize. It screeched like an owl, only much louder.

Suddenly lights were on them, and they were brighter than the sun. Loveland Frog and Loveland Toad froze.

There were more strange noises. Then two creatures came out of the light. They were looking at Loveland Frog and Loveland Toad. It was hard to tell, but Loveland Frog suspected these were the naked hands of the creatures who had transformed him and his friend.

"What should we do?" whispered Loveland Toad.

Loveland Frog wondered. "We should run," he said.

Loveland Toad nodded.

They went as fast as they could. They were not hopping anymore but running, like one of the horses Loveland Frog could see in the distance from the swamp. Their legs seemed to move by themselves. Loveland Frog had not realized how much power he carried in his big body. He thought of himself as the same frog he always was, just bigger. It was then that he knew he was different.

When they had gotten close enough, the scent of the swamp lured them back. "I am so glad we are home!" Loveland Toad exclaimed.

Loveland Frog nodded. "Me too."

IT WAS ANOTHER BRIGHT MORNING. Even though he was tired, Loveland Frog woke at daylight. He yawned and stretched. His back felt strange this morning.

Loveland Toad was already standing on the shore. "Good morning, Loveland Frog," he said. "How was your sleep?"

Loveland Frog could not help smiling. "I slept well. And you?"

"Very well, thank you," said Loveland Toad.

After a breakfast of wiggling creatures, Loveland Frog and Loveland Toad settled down beside the swamp.

"Do you think we should adventure today?" Loveland Frog asked. He was nervous about Loveland Toad's answer, even though he didn't know what his friend would say.

Loveland Toad seemed as if he were thinking. "I am not sure. We do not want to get lost again."

Loveland Frog nodded in agreement. "Getting lost was scary."

They looked beyond the pond at the field. The big animals milled about on the grass. Loveland Frog wondered how different he would be if he were a cow or a horse. He would have always been big. He would have always known how to run from danger.

"What do you think those creatures were?" Loveland Toad asked.

Loveland Frog thought back to the night. All he had seen were those naked hands. He did not want to upset Loveland Toad by bringing up the night they changed. "I am not sure," he said.

"What do you think they were doing in that strange place?"

Loveland Frog watched the sky. The sun was climbing higher. "I believe they were lost," he said.

"Like us," Loveland Toad said.

Loveland Frog nodded.

They sat like that for a long while. Then Loveland Toad said, "Shall we go for a swim today?"

"Perhaps we shall," said Loveland Frog. "But I do not want to see the turtle."

"Ah, yes," said Loveland Toad. "The turtle can be very mean. She bit one of my arm feet." Loveland Toad shook his arm for emphasis.

"We will stay away from the turtle," Loveland Frog said.

And with that, they headed for the water.

# CURVES

Every morning, I pinch my fat. We have this big mirror in the bathroom that spans the length of the wall. When I get out of the shower, all I can see are those rolls pressing against my belly. They've gotten bigger and bigger over the years. I pinch them hard, wishing I could slice them off.

My mother sits at my kitchen table, her lips tense around the rim of a teacup, appraising me with those eyes of hers. I'm waiting for her to insult me as I steep my own bag. Earl Grey, hot.

She takes a delicate sip, then puts her cup down. "Have you been taking your diabetes medicine?"

Yep. There it is.

"Of course. Why wouldn't I be?"

She wrinkles her nose, waves a hand. "Oh, you know. How are your sugars?"

"Fine. At least at my last appointment." Type II, born along with my son—gestational diabetes that never went away.

"You can't get complacent about it because your last A1C was good. Think of your grandmother."

My mother is thin, almost skeletal. Her hair is smooth, no frizz, bouncy. Expertly highlighted. Shiny pink acrylic nails. Botox and retinol keeping her face unlined. You can only tell her age from her neck, bony and wrinkled. Even she can't escape the inevitable march of time. Me? I'm sad. I have never liked my body, and I'm afraid I never will.

My grandmother's sugars were quite high when she died. She also had deadly leukemia. But I'm not going to bring that up.

"It's no problem, Mom. Everything's fine." I realized I've left my tea steeping too long. I lift the bag out and fling it into the trash, a little too hard, then grab half-and-half out of the fridge.

She raises an eyebrow. "Cream, Jessie? Really?"

"Whatever." I don't like the way I sound, like I'm fourteen instead of forty.

"And Lucky Charms in the pantry? I took the liberty of throwing them out. The kids shouldn't be eating that trash. You'll have to wait a while till the replacements get here, though. I ordered that new no-sugar, gluten-free cereal. What is it called?"

"Cardboard?" The fridge door escapes my fingers and slams shut.

She pulls out her iPhone and taps on it. "Oh, no. I think it's called Virtuous."

I lean my head against a cupboard and exhale.

ANOTHER DAY HALFWAY COMPLETED.

My coworker Lainey frowns at me across our lunch table in the cafeteria. I didn't know what to get, so I settled on a protein bar and water. Lainey is eating a big salad. A plastic-wrapped cookie sits aside for later.

"You need to cut her out of your life." Lainey pierces a lettuce leaf and forks it into her mouth.

"I would if I could. Believe me." I've already finished the protein bar and am sipping my water. "You know how it is with childcare."

Lainey rolls her eyes. "Good point. Ours is more than our mortgage."

Her husband works a regular nine to five. He has a nice salary. They can afford things. You feel good walking into Lainey's house. It smells like cherry candles and sleek wood. There is room to move around.

"Same. I can't send them to day care every day. Especially the baby. Do you know how much babies cost these days?"

"I can't even imagine. It was high when my girls were little." Lainey sighs. "I'm so sorry, Jess. I know you're doing everything you can. Terrence is applying everywhere still?"

She chews. I take another drink, longer this time. I wonder what it would be like to eat whatever I wanted whenever I wanted. Envy rises in me as I eye the cookie. Double chocolate.

"Yeah." I move my gaze deliberately down to my fingers, bitten and chewed. My husband lost his job more than a year ago and is working at Home Depot. Schedule all over the damn place. I don't actually know if he is applying for other jobs. I gave up doing everything for him a long time ago.

Lainey brightens. "So if he gets something, you'll be okay. Bye, Mom!"

I wish I could say goodbye to the woman who lives rent-free in my head. "That would be nice," is all I say to Lainey.

Terrence is back by the time I get home. He's made dinner, and the house is picked up. I guess that's one good thing about the retail job. He has more free time during the week. I embrace him from behind, inhaling the sea-salt scent of his soap. He's just out of the shower, still damp. He turns around and kisses me.

We eat the lasagna and talk about our days. I feel bad about eating carbs, but I can't ignore Terrence's work. He puts Wesley to bed while I nurse the baby and hear my mother's thoughts in my head. *You're still breastfeeding? She's nearly eighteen months. Don't you think you should let that go?*

When they're both asleep, we slump down onto the couch. "You okay?" Terrence asks.

"Just tired." I rub my eyes. It's the same conversation we have every night.

He peers at me. "Something's up with you."

"It's nothing." It really is. The same old thing I've fought with since I was a little girl. Since she told me I was getting chubby in the fourth grade. Since she limited what I could eat and made me exercise before I could have dinner. I'd bounce up and down on the first step of the carpeted staircase. Twenty minutes every night.

"Are you upset that I haven't found a job yet?" He examines his hands, rough from moving lumber and heavy carts. "I swear, I've been looking."

"I know." I also know he hasn't been trying that hard. But I'm done with sending him jobs and agonizing over his applications. It's too much.

"Is there anything I can do to help?"

I shake my head.

"Well, let me send you this article I found." Terrence plucks his phone off the table and taps it. My phone is still in my purse, but I feel it vibrate from across the room. "There's a new yoga studio open downtown. Maybe you could take a night off and go?"

Ah, yes. Self-care. The mantra of all parenting books. Put on your oxygen mask first. "I've never really been into that," I say.

"It's worth a try. I get my schedule tomorrow—I'll see when I'll be home in the evening. The place isn't too far from your office."

"I'll think about it." I bite my lip and grab the remote. It's time to zone out.

~

THE NEXT DAY, Terrence has an opening shift. My mother shows up in her Lululemon, hair in a messy bun. She could be an influencer of a certain age. I'm rushing around, the usual morning, throwing lunch and pump parts into my bag. "You should get up earlier," she observes.

At least she's sweet to the kids. I only ever see her smile when she's picking up Emily and hugging her close. I don't blame her there. They're hard at this stage, but it's worth it for those little giggles and wide-eyed wonder. I leave her with them and book it to work.

Lainey meets me in the parking deck with a latte. "You're the best," I sigh. I'll have to make up for the carbs in the milk at lunchtime.

She winks. "No worries. I've got more time with my kiddos at school anyway. I wanted to do something nice for you."

We're a little early. It feels good to slow down as we cross the bridge from the parking deck into the building.

"Any progress with your mom?" Lainey asks carefully.

So this is it. The latte motivation. "Not really."

"What terrible thing did she say today?"

The building smells like new furniture. Our office was renovated last year. It was a pain at the time but is pretty nice now. I have a little cube back in the corner, and Lainey sits on the other side. It's like our little oasis.

"Oh, nothing bad," I say breezily.

Lainey raises an eyebrow. "I'm worried about you, Jess."

"Why?"

"I don't think you realize how burned out you are."

I shrug as I round the corner to my desk. "Isn't this how it is?"

ON THE WAY out to the garage after work, Lainey tells me she's going to a fitness class. I suppress a groan.

"Have you heard of this place? Ladies' Night Fitness?"

I shake my head. Our heels echo on the concrete floor. A soft breeze wafts underneath the walls. It's cooler in here.

"My sister says it's amazing. I'm meeting her there at seven. You wanna come?"

The baby needs to be fed, and I'd have to rush and find gym clothes. "I don't know."

"At least next time." Lainey puts on an exaggerated frown as we approach our cars. "Wouldn't Terrence take care of the kids for you? If it's as good as Bonnie says it is?"

I open the passenger side of my Santa Fe and throw my stuff on the seat: pump bag, cooler, giant purse. "He actually said he heard about a class that was really good."

"Maybe it's the same one!" Lainey brightens. "We'll leave your car here. I'll drive."

IT IS, indeed, the same class Terrence was talking about. I text him on the way home and he's like *good for you!*

Lainey buzzes me home. I feed the baby and we drop off the pumped milk. Athletic wear is the bigger challenge. I moan from my closet while Lainey holds the baby and giggles. "Don't laugh!" I yell back, tossing clothes left and right. I finally come up with an old sports bra and some worn-out leggings. I don't know how I'm supposed to focus on self-care when everything is a blur.

We pull into the parking lot of a nondescript strip mall. Every store is covered by a long blue awning topped by unassuming brick. LADIES NIGHT FITNESS is sculpted in neon letters above the studio. It's next to a Subway and a Drug Mart.

Lainey's sister, Bonnie, stands in front waiting for us. Smaller and more compact than Lainey, Bonnie is gorgeous, a shining example of what regular exercise and responsible eating should do for a person. Her brown hair is pulled into a bun with dangling soft strands, and her pale skin already looks flushed.

"I am so glad you both came!" Bonnie exclaims, hugging her sister. I give her an awkward wave.

"Jess's husband told her about this. Can you believe it?" Lainey gestures to the glass doors. "It has to be good."

"More than good." Bonnie leans forward and opens a door for us. "It's everything."

The studio smells like plastic mats and lavender. A white woman with gray hair wound into a braid greets us. She stands behind a sleek white register and credit card reader. "New here?" she asks me and Lainey.

"First class," Lainey answers.

"Excellent. It's on us today!" She reaches her hand out to grab mine. Her hand is small and smooth. I could break it if I squeezed hard enough. "I'm Denise," she says.

Lainey shakes Denise's hand and turns to me. "This is so awesome!"

I don't feel awesome. More like scared and confused.

Once the clock hits seven, Denise locks the front door and draws a set of black curtains over the glass walls. There are ten of us under the fluorescent lights. I'm sitting on a purple mat, my legs crossed one over the other, painfully aware of the fat oozing over my waistband.

Denise claps her hands. "I'm so glad you are all here. Let's begin!"

There is a low murmur. Bonnie turns to us and grins.

Before the kids, I liked yoga. I would go at least once a week, which is probably why Terrence suggested it. He was working his old job then, managing a small plumbing company, and his hours were regular. He'd reach for the XBOX controller as soon as he saw me in my yoga clothes, and we'd smile at each other.

Now I bend and stretch along with everyone else, slightly out of rhythm, but the moves are still in my limbs. I feel my body opening, letting the thoughts drop from my mind. As we move, my chest tightens with emotion. There's so much I've missed.

THE CLASS IS over before it's begun. I check my phone; it's almost eight. My guess is we'll go into savasana for a few minutes. That will be nice if I don't fall asleep.

Denise gets up and turns the lights down. With the curtains over the front wall to the outside, it's dark save for a soft green light.

"This is the best part," Bonnie whispers.

"For those who have not been here before, this might feel a little odd," Denise says, her voice still singing after instructing for nearly an hour. "I'll light some incense, and then the real transformation will begin. Go with it and be with your body."

Everyone sits. I haven't moved like that for years, so I'm a bit sore. And a little bummed that we're not lying down. That was always my favorite part, the ground holding me up, breathing into the space above me.

I close my eyes. The air does smell different. A mix of cloves and cinnamon, but a different scent underneath. Something darker, anise or coriander. Denise puts on soft music, water rushing beneath piano arpeggios.

I hear the collective breath exhaling from the women.

My skin pops out of its shell around my body. Fleshy pops emanate from around the room. Fear lances up my back, except I don't have a back anymore. My spine has melted. Gobs of tissue expel from my stomach, followed by long, squishy tentacles.

Denise says, "Shhhh. It's all right now."

My eyes are covered with a thin film, like I'm looking through cellophane. Everyone around me has turned into an octopus-like creature. We have alarming green skin and smaller tentacles dripping from our mouths. Our longer ones are easy to flail, moving up and down, new appendages ready to serve us. Below the wet skin, there are rows of yellowish suckers.

"Now is the time to let our human bodies go," Denise says. Her voice has deepened into a low rumble. "We experience a different form of life. We transcend our former selves to move past the insecurities of our flesh."

A strange peace hangs over me as my panic dissipates. I feel utterly in tune with this body. I love the way my belly hangs over the mat, how I can wave my slimy tentacles into the air. I even love the fishy odor that has arrived, mixing with the spices that presumably turned us into these. These creatures who feel nothing but confidence. Sea dominators who could destroy a fleet of ships, pulling the sailors under.

Before I know it, I'm retracting. The air changes again. Everything has snapped back into my usual skin, my usual fat hanging back where it was. The women are all standing, carefully removing themselves from the lingering slime.

"How was it?" Terrence yells from the living room as I stagger through the back door.

I haven't fully processed what happened. So I just yell, "Good!"

He's on the couch with the TV on, Emily slung over his lap. Wes must be in bed already. I slump next to Terrence and run a hand down the baby's arm. She's snoring. Her skin is so soft, like touching clouds, a feeling that can't be compared to any other.

He looks over at me with a weak smile. There are dark circles under his eyes. "I hope you got a chance to relax," he says.

There's a twitch in my gut. A sudden guilt. He woke up at five to work all day and then spent all evening taking care of the kids.

"You should have that too," I say softly. "Hang out with the guys."

Terrence shrugs. "Everyone's busy. It's okay."

We sit together while the TV plays some old cartoon from our twenties. When we had the time to sit around and watch dumb shows.

I'm already in the cube farm when Lainey swans in. "Helloooooo!" she sings, handing me my paper cup.

I peer at her, sitting at my computer as she stands over me. "For the last time, you do not need to get me coffee."

"I want to!" Lainey perches in her chair and puts her purse inside her desk, the drawer rattling. "You never have time."

"There's the office Keurig right over there," I say, pointing an elbow in that direction.

She snorts. "Like I'm gonna let you drink watered-down landfill-choking swill when you could be enjoying brew handcrafted by our gainfully employed neighbors."

I roll my eyes and turn back to my screen, but I smile and take a sip.

Behind me, I can feel Lainey looking at the back of my head. Normally this is the time where we fall into our rhythm of working while chatting a little. But this is intense. She isn't tapping or clicking. I swivel back around.

"Don't you feel amazing?" She reaches for my hands. "I didn't know what to think when we left class. But this morning?"

I consider this. "I'm not sure."

"How can you not be sure!" It's not a question. Lainey squeezes and I feel like my fingers might break. "It's like we're superhuman. We've changed."

She's right about that. I let her hands go and contemplate for a moment under her eager stare. How do I feel?

Peeled wide open and turned inside out. Like an ancient power is welling up inside me, its momentum pulling me forward. I am different. I am remarkable.

～

My mother's signature scent chokes the house.

I put my things down and find her in the living room with the kids. The baby is on the floor with a mountain of board books stacked around her. Wesley is watching *Bluey*, kicking his heels against the frame of the couch. My mother is on her phone, pink tongue sticking out of her clenched face.

She jumps when she finds me. "You're home early."

"Not really. You must have been otherwise preoccupied." I incline my head towards the phone. "Everyone behaved themselves?"

"They are fine." She stands up and brushes back her curls. "They both slept. Two hours in the afternoon."

"That's good." I plunk down next to the baby, and she squeals.

My mother eyes me. "I know that's a struggle for you."

I tilt my head as the baby starts climbing my leg. "What's that?"

"Getting them to nap."

In the past, I have shared this with her. Right now, I don't know what she means. "No, we haven't had any issues."

"You've been complaining since Wesley was a baby." My mother's face is stormy. "Are you okay? You seem off. Oh God, you haven't been drinking, have you? You're still nursing. You should have weaned her a long time ago. Then maybe that kind of thing would be acceptable."

"No! It was a nice day at work." I stand up, the baby pressed to my hip, and turn on my highest-wattage smile. "So, you'll be going now?"

# GREENER GRASS

*I*t's the start of a video. The frozen screen shows two white men waiting for the camera to roll. They sit in front of a backdrop of oak shelves stuffed with books. They both wear checked button-downs and jeans. One is tall and lanky, easy in his body. Salt-and-pepper hair, jaw that could cut glass, wire-rimmed glasses. The other man is shorter, blonder. Stocky but well-built. Slightly smirking at his audience.*

BLOND MAN (*enthusiastically*): Hello all! Welcome back to our show. I'm Joshua, and this is Greg. We're husbands!

GREG (*dryly*): Indeed we are.

JOSHUA: If you're here, you already know what our channel is about. *He whispers.* Cryptids!

GREG *raises an eyebrow at the viewers.*

JOSHUA: C'mon, Greg. You don't have to be all snotty about it.

GREG (*huffy*): I said I would be in the video, didn't I?

JOSHUA (*turning back to the camera*): Yes. We'll see how long he participates.

GREG *frowns.* JOSHUA *places his hands in his lap.*

JOSHUA: Anyway. I thought we'd tell the story that got us here in the first place. So you know we're not liars. This is for your safety, you know. Cryptids are a very real problem.

GREG: Do we need to explain cryptids to the studio audience?

JOSHUA *(waves a hand)*: No, people watching this should know. They're real fans.

GREG: Will we have a chance to edit things out if we mess up?

JOSHUA: Of course, babe.

GREG: Okay, then. This is for all of you who know precisely what cryptids are. Our story consists of several components, none of which were exciting to experience. But as Joshua said, it's important for you all to understand the gravity of the situation.

JOSHUA *(whispers again)*: Isn't he cute? All those big words. He was valedictorian of his high school class. So adorable, I can't even stand it.

GREG *gives the camera a withering look and continues.*

GREG: Joshua signed us up for a lawn service.

JOSHUA: Babe, I swear I didn't know.

GREG: You have said that a few times.

JOSHUA: I didn't! *(He addresses the camera.)* I was at home minding my business.

GREG: He doesn't work.

JOSHUA: This is not relevant information!

GREG: He thinks he's going to be the next YouTube star.

JOSHUA: OMG, Greg.

GREG: It's important because you're home all day long. We won't tell them about your afternoon Twizzlers and porn habit.

JOSHUA: OMG, stop. *He pushes Greg's elbow and returns to direct address.* Greg and I are in the process of hiring a surrogate for our first child. I'll be the stay-at-home parent, so there's no reason for me to work right now.

GREG: You could get your barista job back.

JOSHUA *(whining)*: My manager doesn't like me! Pronouns they/them, BTW. They said I was taking too many breaks and that if I had time to lean, I had time to clean. What even does that mean? I work for the fun of it, m'kay? I don't need to kiss their butt all the time.

GREG: Must be nice.

JOSHUA: Ooooohkay, Mr. Big Engineer Man.

GREG: If it weren't for me, your problems would no longer be first world.

JOSHUA: Yeah, well, you're way more employable than I am.

GREG: Shall we return to the story?

JOSHUA: We aren't going to have any content left if I have to keep editing this stuff out. *He punches Greg's arm again.* See, I'm contributing! Once this goes viral and I can put ads on it, I'll be raking in the dough and you can retire.

GREG: I think I'll save that plan for a few more decades.

JOSHUA: Anyway! I was sitting at home waiting for Greg. I make dinner for him every day and make sure the house is clean. That's right, I was a fifties housewife in a previous life.

GREG (*ignoring Joshua's babble*): I was at work. Joshua opened the door to this sales rep.

JOSHUA: I should probably tell this part since you weren't there.

GREG *shrugs.*

JOSHUA: So this guy was really short, maybe between four and five feet? I'm five foot four and I towered over him. I didn't realize he was a sales rep. I thought maybe he was a leprechaun. *He claps his hands.* Now, you might be thinking this is where a cryptid shows up. Think again!

GREG *stares at the camera.*

JOSHUA: Okay, he didn't have red hair or rosy cheeks or anything. And he wasn't wearing green. But hey, he should have been because of the product he was selling, huh? He did look tired. Like he was walking around all day and no one was buying.

GREG: You felt sorry for him.

JOSHUA: I totally did.

GREG: We barely have a lawn anyway. And with the baby coming, we don't have the extra money to spend on lawn service.

JOSHUA: With the baby coming, I won't have time to spend on dealing with the lawn.

GREG: Yet you have time to record this video.

JOSHUA: Because this video is going to go viral and we are going to make tons of money on it. And then we will have the money to pay for a lawn service. Like, a different one.

GREG: Do you seriously think you can keep up this channel after staying up all night with the baby?

JOSHUA: I know, okay! It's gonna be a big change. *He worries his lips with his teeth.* Let's get back to the story. The guy was short and weird-looking. Maybe he was a troll or something. He seemed sad. Like he had lost something on the way to work. Or he got the wrong order at lunch.

GREG: Or he didn't sell anything that day because the product was —is—subpar.

JOSHUA: Going to the Better Business Bureau is not part of this series. *He turns to Greg.* Do you think it should be?

GREG: We'll see.

JOSHUA *(pouting)*: We'll see always means no!

GREG: Let's see how this video does. *He softens.* My dear.

JOSHUA: Awwww. You do have feelings.

GREG: Focus. Dear.

JOSHUA: You're the one who keeps derailing us. *He turns back to the camera.* Long story short. The guy said the company could get our beige grass greener.

GREG: It's not really beige.

JOSHUA: Whatever. Not green. The rep said because they work at night, the team can get more water on the grass or something like that. It gets dry here, you know. This is really a desert, like we're in a desert valley.

GREG: Most places here don't even have grass. It's rocks and shrubs.

JOSHUA: Way to rub it in. Yes, we still have grass. No, I don't want grass anymore after all this. I never want to see a blade of grass again.

GREG: I promise I'll work on it on paternity leave.

JOSHUA *(scoffing)*: You think we're going to have any time for you to mess around in the yard? You were the one who said I wouldn't have time because of the baby.

GREG: This channel is about cryptids.

JOSHUA: Okay. Back to the cryptids. So, where the cryptids come in is after I signed the contract.

GREG: He signed the contract without checking with me. I was not happy.

JOSHUA: "Not happy" is an understatement.

GREG: I have a spreadsheet of our expenses and subscriptions. This isn't in our budget. And he signed a contract for a whole year. So I couldn't cancel.

JOSHUA: But you tried.

GREG: I told the man on the phone that you weren't thinking straight when you talked to him. He wouldn't hear any of it.

JOSHUA: From now on I won't sign anything unless there's a notary and a witness.

GREG: I was mad at you. But we're on better footing now, I think.

JOSHUA: Now that we got our money back. So that takes us back to our encounter with… (*whispers*) the Fresno Nightcrawler.

GREG: Multiple Fresno Nightcrawlers.

JOSHUA: Greg would never have believed this if he didn't see it with his own eyes.

GREG: I'm not exactly a convert. I don't have proof of Bigfoot's existence, for example. But yes. I can attest to the truth of my experience with the Nightcrawlers.

JOSHUA: The salesman told me our first treatment would begin that night and would occur daily for the first week, then drop down to weekly and then monthly. So I knew to expect them. I was going to go outside and say hello, but I didn't make it past midnight. I fell asleep before they showed.

GREG: I didn't see a difference.

JOSHUA: I told you it takes time. Rome wasn't built in a day.

GREG: That is as dumb a phrase as *if you have time to lean, you have time to clean.*

JOSHUA (*clapping*): Ouch. Maybe I should go back to Starbucks.

GREG: The next day was even worse.

JOSHUA: I'm not saying it wasn't bad! It was bad! The whole experience was bad!

GREG: The next day there were holes all over the lawn.

JOSHUA: I called. The rep said they dug the holes so the extra water could seep into the ground.

GREG: I'm an engineer. This explanation did not sit well with me.

JOSHUA: Sit *well*? LOL.

GREG: Must you continue speaking in text messages?

JOSHUA *(shrugging)*: A little pun shouldn't hurt anything.

GREG: That was day two.

JOSHUA: Day three was when it got weird.

GREG: There were more and more pockmarks in the grass. Almost like footsteps the way they were patterned.

JOSHUA *(pointing a thumb at Greg)*: He was the one who called the next day.

GREG: I talked to the owner. The rep wasn't doing us any good.

JOSHUA: Greg said we would get part of our money back.

GREG: The owner said the workers were slacking.

JOSHUA: He said "That's what you get when you can't find good help."

GREG: So we were supposed to get our money back.

JOSHUA *(putting on a shocked face)*: Spoiler!

GREG *(frowning)*: We did not.

*Silence for a beat.*

JOSHUA: They were still coming every night. Our grass was trampled into oblivion. And the owner wasn't giving us our money back.

GREG: I did consider going to the Better Business Bureau at that point. But we decided to get cameras first.

JOSHUA *(leaning forward, propping his chin on one arm, his arm propped on his knee)*: Greg went to get cameras. I stayed up late to stalk them.

GREG: At that point, we did not have footage.

JOSHUA *(splaying jazz hands)*: Does that mean we have footage now?

GREG: You already know the answer to this question, Joshua.

JOSHUA: Uh, yeah, but the audience doesn't. *He looks back at the camera.* Who thinks we got the footage? Gimme a like if you do.

GREG *pauses.*

JOSHUA *smiles and gives a tiny wave.*

GREG: Are we live right now?

JOSHUA *(grinning sheepishly):* Would you be mad if I told you we were?

GREG: You said we could edit this!

JOSHUA: *(pointing at camera)* We can! For the recording. Anyway, everyone out there is expecting me to speak now that my TikTok is viral.

GREG: Your TikTok??

JOSHUA: Yeah. Because you're a square and you're not on it. *He preens.* I will have you know I am TikTok famous. Isn't that right, YouTube?

GREG *squints.*

JOSHUA: Oh, shoot, I need my phone to read your comments. *He sits up and digs in his pocket. Greg is silently fuming.*

*Joshua consults his screen and squeals.* Oh, thanks, sistermister2003! We are styled well today, aren't we? *He reaches up to ruffle Greg's hair, but it's gelled down so much that it can't move. Greg winces at Joshua's touch.*

JOSHUA *(frowning)*: Okay, mothmanluv22. First of all, Mothman is soooooo overrated. Second of all, how dare you question us? *He reads and rolls his eyes.* I guess you're right. I didn't say whether or not we do have the footage. *(in a stage whisper)* You won't have to wonder anymore... after a word from our sponsors.

GREG: What are you doing? I can't believe you did this without consulting me.

JOSHUA: I'm the Internet's sweetheart!

GREG: Besides the YouTube thing, you should have told me about the video. You're out there talking about our private circumstances to the whole world?

JOSHUA: We have been swindled. And the perpetrators ought to know that millions of people are out there making sure we don't get swindled again. *He side-eyes the camera.*

GREG: Are we still live??

JOSHUA: Um, I can't actually tell when the ads are going to come up? It's, like, random.

GREG *gets up and puts his head into his hands. He mutters and paces.*

GREG: I went to school to be an engineer. I was supposed to be an engineer and nothing else.

JOSHUA: Are you still with us, baby? *He bats his eyelashes.*

GREG *(sighing):* I suppose I have nothing to lose at this time. *He peers at the camera.* This better be worth it.

JOSHUA *(consulting his phone)* : Ooooh, Greg, adventuretime1000 thinks you are super hot. The man behind the... hey! I don't appreciate that, adventuretime1000.

GREG: Let's get back to the story. Although I suppose your fans know exactly what happened by now.

JOSHUA: The TikTok does kinda give it away.

GREG: Can you just show me the TikTok?

JOSHUA *swipes on his phone.*

JOSHUA: Okay, okay.

*He holds the phone out to Greg. Tinny sounds come from the phone and carry into the video.*

GREG: Okay, so, they definitely know.

JOSHUA: And we're definitely making bank on this! *He flashes his teeth.* If for some reason you're not familiar, I'm the "The Fresno Night-crawler Stole My Money" guy.

GREG: Shall I go back to the part about the cameras?

JOSHUA: Okay, yeah. We got a little ahead of ourselves. So I stayed up late, and that was the first time I saw them. *He pauses, then resumes in a hushed tone.* It was freaky. It's exactly like you've seen online. White creatures, almost translucent. Smaller than you'd think, and faster. They move so fast they practically leave a smoke trail behind them. No torso, just a head and legs, and those legs are fucking sharp, fam.

GREG: At this time I was not completely sold on the cryptid idea. I had gone to bed.

JOSHUA: TBH, babe, I had no clue there were cryptids involved. All I knew was that some jackass had sold me greener grass and we did not have greener grass.

GREG: And the next time I called, the owner told me I was an idiot for thinking Fresno could have green grass in the first place. I'm not even the one who signed the contract.

JOSHUA: As you keep reminding me.

GREG: That is when we got the cameras.

JOSHUA: And the footage. Which we will play for you now.

*He presses a button on his phone, and the video starts.*

GREG: Can they hear us while the video is going?

JOSHUA: No more sassy talk now that we can't edit.

GREG: We could never edit.

JOSHUA: I said we can for the archive!

GREG: You didn't tell me we would be live.

JOSHUA: Well, maybe I wanted you to get the short end for a change.

GREG: What do you mean by that?

JOSHUA: I mean, you didn't tell me that the surrogate with Chloe didn't work out.

GREG: You honestly want to air this dirty laundry in front of—*he waves a hand toward the camera*—the entire Internet?

JOSHUA: I muted the mic. *He shakes the phone in his hand.*

GREG: You did not. You're such a liar.

JOSHUA: I wouldn't bring up Chloe in front of all these people. Trust.

GREG: I don't believe you. *He looks at the camera.* Fine, Internet. Are you happy now? Joshua and I can't have a kid, at least not until we find someone who will carry it for us. Maybe one of you wants to do it! Give us a call now that we're Internet famous!

*The room is quiet.*

JOSHUA *(voice trembling):* And we're back.

GREG: So... you've seen what we got. I suppose there's only one part of the story left.

JOSHUA: So far.

GREG: I sent the footage to the owner. He laughed at me. They had run their course with us and told me I would eventually get my money back.

JOSHUA: We did not.

GREG: We've established that.

JOSHUA: And this is when I made the TikTok.

GREG: Joshua only knew about the bank statements because I pointed it out. He doesn't read the bank statements. He stays home and eats bonbons.

JOSHUA: I do not! I take good care of this house. See if you get dinner tomorrow.

GREG: At least I have money to go buy takeout.

JOSHUA *hisses and draws back.*

JOSHUA: You monster.

GREG: Anyway, that's how the Fresno Nightcrawlers stole all our money.

JOSHUA: So you actually don't have the money to pay for takeout.

GREG: I'm being dramatic.

JOSHUA: *(shocked)* You? Dramatic? Never.

GREG: We are on stage here, aren't we?

JOSHUA: So do we have money or not? Besides our ad revenue. *He peeks at his phone.* OMG, Greg, we're losing viewers. They must think we're full of shit.

GREG: You all want your own little nightcrawlers for your lawn?

JOSHUA: Or your excuse for a lawn?

GREG: I've got their phone number right here. I've got them on camera. I've got them under my goddamn fingers. So anyone who thinks we're bullshitting can get the fuck out.

JOSHUA: Oh, dear. Darling, I think you need a break from this. *He faces the camera.* Well, my loves, I hate to leave you, but I hope you'll join us for our next video! We'll be talking about Chupacabra, I think, if I can get the perfect guest.

*The video winks off.*

～

GREG SLUMPS IN HIS CHAIR. "God, that was exhausting."

Joshua is bouncing in his seat. "Are you kidding? It was perfect. I can't wait to see our bank account once that sweet sweet revenue hits it."

"At this point, I don't even care." Sweat beads on Greg's brow, and he mops it with his checkered shirt sleeve. "What are you making for dinner?"

"You don't want to pay for takeout?" Joshua asks with a sly smile.

"Do I have a choice?"

"I gotta keep the locals happy."

They order pizza. Greg gets thin crust and a big salad. Joshua opts for the meat lovers' with garlic bread and wings. "Meat lovers," he says with a wink over the food. Greg rolls his eyes.

As the sun goes down, they open a bottle of wine.

"I'm still upset, you know," Joshua says. "About Chloe."

Greg studies his glass of red before taking a long swallow.

"Why didn't you tell me? Was it really because I didn't inform you about the grass thing?"

Greg blinks. "No. Not at all. I... didn't know how to tell you."

It's Joshua's turn to stay silent. He puts his wineglass down on the coffee table and entwines his fingers.

"Hey, listen." Greg turns to Joshua and puts a gentle hand under his chin. "We're going to make it work, okay? We're on so many lists. And you just told the entire Internet that we need a surrogate. Someone's gotta come forward. Right?"

Joshua laughs, and it's enough to let the tears go. He sniffles. "Right."

"I love you. You know that, right?" Greg slips his arm around Joshua and pulls him close. It's a quick dance as Joshua rearranges himself against Greg's chest.

They sit like that for a while.

Eventually, Greg gets up and starts putting the food away. "I'm going to get on the Peloton for a while," he says. "You gonna be okay?"

Joshua stands up quickly. "Oh, yeah, babe. I'll be fine. Can you just leave some of that meat lovers' out? I'm still hungry."

～

THE VALLEY IS COOLER at night. Joshua steps into the backyard, holding the pizza box, and lets the air wash over his face. It's a balm to his scratched-up soul.

He's made sure the camera is off. "Come on now," he whispers.

It's enough for them to hear him. They crowd around his feet, soft furry creatures with big liquid eyes. He can't resist the nightcrawlers. He loved them from the moment he saw them in the yard. He wished he'd known them all those nights before.

Joshua pets as many heads as he can while doling out the surplus slices. They trill, sweet sounds of gratitude. He admires them as they make off with the pizza and dip back out into their hiding places. Wherever it is they hide.

So what if they were part of a slimy scheme. They didn't know. They were only doing what their shitty bosses told them. The nightcrawlers are victims, Joshua knows. He's saving them. Taking care of them. This is what he's meant to do, after all. He's never happy if he's not pleasing someone. It's not the same as it could be, but it works for now.

He pushes down a surge of love and whispers that he'll see them tomorrow. Then he turns his back on the lush green grass behind him.

# DEVIL THIRTEEN

The comments started around number four.

"Don't you know what causes that?"

"I don't know how you do it!"

"You've got an entire football team!"

By the twelfth, Joan was used to the stares. They rarely went out as an entire family; they had to use the big van, and it was impossible to get the babies in while the others horsed around in the back. It had to be done once a week for church, but she preferred to take only a few of the children out to the Wawa. The oldest, Judith, was responsible enough to take care of the others with help from Maribeth and Liliana, the older twins.

They lived forty minutes from Barnegat Township. Bill had wanted a rural home. Taxes were lower here. Pines towered all around them. As the children multiplied, they needed more space.

"Do you mix them up?" people asked.

Joan wanted to ask them if they remembered the names of all their cousins, all their coworkers. Each one of her children was special, precious. For others, they might blur into one big mass of similar faces, but Joan knew each one of her children by heart.

As much as she loved them all, Joan did not want another child.

She was approaching her forties. She had been nursing or pregnant or both for half her life. The church did not believe in birth control, so Joan's only tactic was to stay away from Bill during her fertile times.

She dreamed of her impossible escape. She'd wake in the middle of the night gasping for breath because she wanted it so badly.

It wouldn't work, though. The church would pursue her. She'd seen it: Eloise Tyler, who had seven children, ran away from home and never returned. Richard Tyler had a new wife within a few months. Joan was disposable too.

Even dispatching Bill—as crazy as it sounded—wouldn't work. The elders would find another husband for Joan. She'd continue bearing children until she was worn out, her nipples leaking for the rest of her life, her uterus shifting and falling, her body wrecked.

So eventually, inevitably, Bill cornered her at the wrong time.

THE TEST WAS NOT SO MUCH a surprise as a sentence.

She'd returned from the store trailed by her older twins, each of them toting a baby twin. The bulk items were still in the van, but Joan slung the plastic bag containing the pregnancy test and some mascara onto the kitchen table. "Oh, are these your grandchildren?" the teen at the register had cooed in the Dollar Tree, clearly not paying attention to the items in Joan's basket.

"Kids!" Joan yelled. "I need help!"

The lot of them came tumbling down the stairs. Bill had trained them well—any resistance would lead to punishment. The ones still nursing were exempt, but once weaned, the children were on their own when it came to behavior. She wanted to shield them so badly, wanted to pull them away from him and hold them, but his word was law.

Today, she was happy that they obeyed, that they hauled in the groceries with no complaint. Today, she needed peace.

The children would have rest time: the younger ones napping, the older ones with their Bibles, drawing, or reading. Joan, too, would often study her Bible. As an assistant pastor, Bill worked from home. The church helped to subsidize their living. But this meant that Joan never had time away from him. Not a second. "Women are meant to be watched," Bill would say. "They will be tempted otherwise. Look at Eve."

Joan wished she had Eve's courage.

When the house was quiet, she peed on the stick and got the answer she didn't want. She stared at the two familiar pink lines and whispered: *Let this child be set free.*

SHE HADN'T NEEDED a pregnancy test at all; the vomiting had already started. As soon as those cells merged, Joan would become tender. Her breasts and cervix and hips ached; her stomach turned alien. Nothing she ate would stay down, not even ginger ale. She survived on crackers and water.

On Sunday night, the house lost power. Their remote location meant that the men of the church would have to work in concert to bring it back. Most of the grid came from turbines and solar. When the kids whined, Bill said, "You are fortunate to be blessed by what we have. Imagine always living without these conveniences."

When the power came back, he left it off for a week. He stayed locked in the bedroom that doubled as an office with only a candle to light his desktop. Bill toiled over a notebook, scratching pencil across reams of paper, coming out only to use the bathroom. Meanwhile, Joan and the children fought without washer and dryer and dishwasher, without running water, without working toilets. Bill didn't believe in disposable diapers. Joan vomited in the trees as she used Dawn and dirty river water to clean her children's clothing.

When he turned the power back on, she wanted to sleep for a week.

He announced himself transformed. "I have seen God," he said. "All of you should retreat from the grid. Electricity and plumbing have turned us into fools. We take these luxuries for granted. God cannot speak to us when we are thus distracted."

Many of the families turned their power off for days, weeks, months. Joan could never know when it would happen. There was no warning: Bill would simply shut the power down when he felt the family was becoming too comfortable.

SHE HAD to be extra careful.

She'd heard rumors. A woman lived not too far from her, in a cabin near one of the small lakes that pooled in the woods. The church women called her a witch, but they used the word in a different fashion, an almost reverent tone.

Joan went by herself on a Sunday. She told Bill she had morning sickness and couldn't go to church. He lectured her at first, but then she threw up on his boots.

She felt terrible about asking the older girls to care for the younger ones while she wandered in the woods, her muck boots sinking into the swampy soil. She depended on them far too much. It wasn't fair to them. Thinking about this made her stomach hurt, and she threw up again on the side of the path. There was hardly anything left in her belly, and the acid of the bile corroded her throat.

The house was small, but not really a cabin as the other women had described it. There was a gravel driveway leading out to the road, and a rusty red truck sat in a makeshift parking space. The lake shimmered beside the building; the grass and garden were well-tended. Joan's heart pounded as she knocked.

The woman came to the door. She didn't open it all the way, but Joan glimpsed her: white skin, long blonde hair like cornsilk. "I'm sorry, who is it?"

"My name's Joan. I'm sorry to bother you. I didn't know how to contact you."

The woman chuckled. "Ah, that happens a lot. Please give me a moment—I'm not dressed. I'll put some coffee on."

Joan waited outside. She wrapped her arms around herself and swayed. The acid still burned in her throat. She worried about getting back to the house on time.

The door swung open again, fully this time. The woman's hair was swept into a ponytail now. She wore loose jeans and a flannel top, fully at ease with her surroundings. "I'm Eden," she said, ushering Joan inside. "Let's talk, shall we?"

Joan perched on the edge of a faded, threadbare couch while Eden puttered in the kitchen. The rich scent of Eden's coffee filled the room, but Joan had no interest. Maybe Eden saw Joan's face, because she said, "Or would you rather have tea?"

Joan's voice broke. "Tea would be great."

Eden nodded and got to work filling a kettle. Joan looked around, not sure where to land her gaze. The house did have cabin-like finishings, lots of light log wood and a spiraling staircase that led to a loft. There was a bathroom hall behind the kitchen—good to know in case she needed to throw up again. The chaos in Joan's stomach could easily lead to that.

Eden approached Joan with a steaming mug. "It's chamomile. I hope that's okay. It usually helps with the queasiness."

Joan took it carefully. "It's exactly what I need."

"I can dump out the coffee if it's too much for you." Eden sat across from her in an equally sagging armchair. "I should have known better, but you'll have to forgive me—I just woke up."

"No, it's okay. I am on a timetable, though."

"I thought so."

The warm tea helped Joan's aching throat. She explained as swiftly as she could. Eden nodded, as if she'd heard the story a hundred times before.

As Joan finished, she pulled her hands to her face, resting her palms on her burning cheeks.

Eden spoke gently. "It sounds like you have a connection to this child. Is that true?"

"I'm not sure." Joan blinked away tears. "The women said you have a way to..."

"I have many ways. But yes, that is one of them if you want that option." Eden gestured to Joan's mug. "I would never deceive you into one of the special teas. They're as soothing as the chamomile, at least until the bleeding starts."

Eden stretched out a hand. Joan set her already cooling mug on an end table and let the woman pull her up. Silently, she followed Eden through the kitchen and down the hall that adjoined it. One room, as Joan had expected, was closed off—the bathroom. But at the end of the hall, Eden pushed open another door.

Joan took it in, felt a sense of wonder. The space was filled: a huge bathtub in one corner, a large plastic ball and bed in another. Machines sat beside the bed, and cabinetry lined the walls. The whole place smelled like vanilla.

"I'm a midwife," Eden said. "This is the birthing room."

Joan put a hand to her chest. She'd labored with her children at home, surrounded by women from the church. They held her hand through the pain, but she'd never seen anything like this.

"What are you thinking?" Eden asked. "I'm mindful of your timetable."

Joan gasped. She'd already forgotten. "I don't know," she said. "I don't know."

The blonde woman stepped forward, gestured to Joan's belly. "Can I?" Joan didn't even have the words to say no. Eden placed her palm on the mound there. "What do you feel?"

It was the only response that came to Joan's mind. "Consumed."

ONE NIGHT, he caught her crying, balled up in a corner of the bed, making herself as small as she could. "Joanie?" he said.

Joan turned over. Bill rubbed a hand on her shoulder. For a moment he looked like the boy she had married, whose eyes were alight with promise.

"I'm fine," she said, batting him away.

His hand moved down to her leg. Now the heat of it stung her skin under her lacy nightdress. "What's wrong?"

*Everything.* "It's fine. No big deal."

"Oh, Joanie. You need the Lord. Have you been going to women's Bible study?"

*When would I have time?*

"Tell you what. Let's make sure you have a chance to go this week. When is it?"

Her vision blurred with fresh tears. She didn't know. She'd never wanted to.

He patted her and finally removed his hand. "I'll find out. Judith can go with you."

## Judith

Judith was sixteen, but her father had forbidden her from getting a driver's license. All the girls would submit to their husbands when they were of age, and their husbands would decide if they could drive.

So when her mother started feeling dizzy, there was nothing Judith could do.

"Pull over, Mother," she said as the baby twins wailed in the back. "Just take a minute."

Her mother shook her head. "The Bible study is at ten. If we don't make it there, your father will know."

Judith hated her father. Joan's face was deathly pale, her skin taking on a green tint. They were still twenty minutes from the church.

"Please," Judith said. "I'll text him."

Joan veered off the dirt road and landed half in a ditch. Judith's door dangled; she had to crawl into the back to get the babies. She unlatched their weathered child seats and pulled them out one at a time. Her mother was bent over, dry-heaving into the ditch.

Judith shivered. She felt so useless.

Her mother collapsed, her thin legs buckling. Judith screamed and ran to her. She had no words, only her hands on her mother's arms, trying to pull her back up. But her mother was semi-conscious, her head lolling.

Judith gritted her teeth. Cringing, she lay her mother down in the mud, then doubled back to the van for blankets. They kept plenty in case of a breakdown or if the children were cold. Women in church liked to make them as gifts.

She spread out a quilt and pulled her mother onto it. Joan was rousing a little, enough to make her body more pliable, easier to move. Her eyes fluttered between her lashes. Judith knelt beside her, wishing she had water, anything to make her mother more comfortable.

The twins quieted, spent by their own crying. Judith blinked tears out of her eyes. The silence of the pines pushed down on her. The trees felt dead beneath the heavy gray sky.

Her mother coughed and tried to sit up. Judith grabbed her hand, squeezed it. "It's okay, Mother. You don't have to move."

"We need to get to the church."

"I'll call Father. He can borrow Pastor's truck. You don't have to go."

"He'll think we did this on purpose." Joan's breath sped up. Judith's chest went tight, her body mirroring her mother's. "To avoid Bible study. He'll punish us."

"No, no." Flashes of her father, his rage, a belt used as a whip. "I will not let him hurt you. What about the baby?"

"Which one?"

Judith pointed to her mother's belly, low and sagging from the shadows of its former occupants.

Joan cringed. "Your father doesn't know."

"How could he not?" Judith's anger balled up in her like something crazy and alive. She'd begun attending births when she was twelve, had seen her mother grow and labor and shrink and grow again.

Joan leaned her head back. "Maybe it doesn't matter."

Judith considered the blanket below her mother's hips, where blood bloomed and spread.

JOAN SAT on the filthy blanket and nursed the boys one at a time. Her head spun. She felt loose, untethered, like she might float away from her body.

This wasn't actually her body, though. It belonged to everyone else. To her husband, who used it when he liked. To her children, who crawled on her, demanded her attention. To the babies, who sucked out her strength. And the one who occupied her now, as they all did.

Was it still there? She'd lost a lot of blood. Its coppery smell flooded her senses along with the scent of the fresh mud. Her limbs were streaked with red and brown.

But the bleeding had stopped. Joan had lost babies. She would have kept bleeding, would have been possessed by pain. She felt no pain now except for the ache in her stomach.

Judith stood by the road, waving at passing cars. People flew down this road, even with its bumpy rocks-and-dirt surface, and it took some time for someone to stop. But Joan was grateful as she saw a big green truck pull up beside her van. A truck with a hitch.

A tall man got out, beard halfway to his knees, bald head shiny even with no sun. "What's the problem, ladies?"

Judith pointed. "Can you pull us out?"

The man smirked. "For you, I can."

Joan closed her eyes and tried to catch a breath. What mattered was that he had a rope in his truck, a rope that connected to the van, and he could drive his truck so the van came back to ground.

She was shaky. Hungry. They were back in forty minutes. Judith jumped out and ran for the house, her braid bouncing against her denim jumper. She returned with juice and water, pushed it into her mother's hands. The door to the house slammed behind her.

Bill sauntered up to the car, hands in his jean pockets, as if he traded in casual evil. Joan still sat in the driver's seat, the juice at her lips. Bill opened the door, reached in, and pulled the juice away.

"Where have you been?"

She felt the lie on her lips—she'd been at Bible study the whole time, hadn't she? But he would know somehow. He had tracking on her cell phone; he could have called the church. "We got stuck," she said.

"Sure. I got a call from Randy Henderson." Bill took a long swig, grape stain spreading around his lips. He threw the bottle to the ground, and it rolled a few feet. Joan didn't open her water. "Said he pulled you out of a ditch along 72."

"My phone doesn't work there. I couldn't call you."

"Your cell was off." He narrowed his eyes. "What were you doing out there?"

"Just what Randy said." She hadn't recognized the man, but Bill knew everyone in town.

Bill reached into the door and pulled her out bodily, her feet tangling on the drop from seat to ground. "Why?"

"I was sick. Bleeding."

Her hand drifted to her belly. There would be no going back now.

She knew in her gut that the remedy had not worked. Only enough to bring on the blood and the tears. After all she had done to see the midwife, to elude Bill, to avoid his punishment. This was her fate.

Bill drew in a breath. He fell to the stone and grasped her around the waist. Pushed his head into her already hardening belly, kissed it with wet lips against her dress. "Is everything okay now? You didn't lose it?"

Joan shook her head and winced. "Everything's fine."

AT THE NEXT MEETING, Pastor Simeon blessed Joan. He put his hands on her belly, as he always did, and she squirmed. "Let Joan and William's child thrive among his family and that of our church. Let he always be loved in your sight, oh God."

Everyone clapped. Joan stepped off the stage, yielding to the song and prayer that would come next.

She would enter the second trimester soon. The baby would begin to kick and flutter, turning like a fish before it got too big to move much. She liked this part: the quickening, the rising, a clump of cells transforming.

The younger children had their quiet time after church and lunch. The older children curled up in the living room with their books. Laura

Ingalls Wilder for Liliana, an Amish romance for Maribeth, *Jane Eyre* for Judith. Bill insisted upon the classics. Joan rested on the couch, Peter strapped to her, Jonah in the Pack and Play beside her. Bill sat at the dining room table with his laptop, as usual, and Joan closed her eyes.

"Girls, we need to talk."

She jolted awake at the words, half dreaming already. He cleared his throat, putting on his pastor voice.

"Come here. It's time for the three of you to start thinking about betrothal."

They stood. Joan could feel the reluctance in the room.

She thought of her parents. They were dead now, but they'd been ardent members of the church. Joan grew up in a little house a few streets behind it. She'd never been out of Jersey, had never even been to the metropolitan areas of the state.

Her mother was a fragile woman, Joan her only child. The elders fawned over Joan, proclaimed her the Millers' miracle. Sarah Miller had yearned for a bigger family, though, and seemed to resent Joan for daring to be born. As if Joan had held her siblings back, taking the space meant for them.

Joan's betrothed had to be special. She'd thought of him, prayed for him as the elders told her to do. She awaited their romantic courtship. They'd never touch, always be looked after by a wise chaperone, and she'd get to know him like a best friend. When they married, she'd be set on fire for God, ecstatic to be with her lifetime partner.

William Waite fit the bill, so to speak. His family was new to town, new to the faith. They were hungry to know more, to immerse themselves, and the Millers were eager to teach them. Bill and Joan began their courtship on a children's playground, Joan's mother watching from a park bench as if they were toddlers.

Sometimes Joan thought they were better back then, before he could touch her. He talked instead. He was a humble person, didn't have big dreams, but he wanted a good life. She'd hoped to have that life with him.

Now her three girls stood in a row facing their father, their eyes huge and liquid.

"I've been talking to Pastor about our options." Bill sat below them, his belly hanging out over his waistband, as big as Joan's. "Lili, there's a young man at church—you may have met him? He's just out of Bible college. Apprenticing now. Wayne, I believe?"

Joan couldn't picture the boy. Nor could she picture the other one Bill mentioned for Maribeth. They all blurred together, these young white forest boys. Strapping lads with no dreams. Just like Bill.

"For you, Judith, I believe you've already met your match." Bill let out a honking laugh at his own joke. "I've been talking with Randy Henderson."

Joan's eyes flew open. The brute with the truck.

Maribeth and Lili sat back down on the floor. Judith remained standing, staring. The baby dealt her a sharp kick as if protesting.

Judith licked her lips. "Father, I respect you and your thoughts for me, as you are the head of the household." Her voice came out high and stringy. "But I need more time to pray on this."

Bill's gaze moved slowly between Judith and her sisters. "I don't see Lili or Maribeth arguing with me."

"I'm sorry, Father. I don't mean to argue." Judith modulated her tone. "Can you consider waiting until you have established the courtships for my sisters?"

Bill ground his teeth.

Joan held her breath. Her daughters moved like shadows now, whispering, obedient. Only Judith retained some of her spunk. She'd been so energetic, wiggling while Joan brushed her hair, always the first to splash in a mud puddle. Joan cherished those early days when she only had Judith and the older twins. Even with the next baby tucked inside her, she'd savored that time, just her and her girls.

"I will pray upon it," he said, leaning on the pronoun. "I will bring you back the instruction when I have heard the word of God."

That night, he turned off the power again.

JOAN PRAYED. All through her third trimester, all through the sharp kicks and jabs. When her body became too big for her, she prayed. *Don't let him destroy her like the others.* She knew the baby was a girl.

Her heartburn came on like fire. Then her stomach squeezed by her womb, bringing her vomit back. The swelling, the fatigue, her belly always in her way, early labor pains shuddering through her. All the while she cooked, fires made of flint and tinder, huge pots of bubbling soup. The children tired of peanut butter sandwiches, but she had little else to feed them. Her girls helped her string up the diapers. They carried the nurslings, brought her water, helped to wean Eli so there would be room on the breast for the new baby. He was the second youngest child before Peter and Jonah, but Joan could not support four children draining the life from her.

The pain came on strong one night under the full moon. Bill snored like a hacksaw. Joan slipped out of bed. She woke the three girls, careful not to disturb the younger ones. The four of them stumbled through the woods, Joan stopping when the contractions rippled through her. After so many, she didn't have long.

Eden stood at the cabin's door, her smile creasing her face. Joan could barely think. Her body was drugged with pain. Eden resembled an angel, hair tumbling over one shoulder, a glow settling over her skin. "Thank you," Joan said. "Thank you so much."

"We knew she'd come fast. I have everything set up for you." Eden gestured behind her. Joan stepped heavily into the living room, the girls scurrying in after. A massive plastic tub lay there, undulating with water. Joan craved the heat, the warmth, all the comfort that would bring her baby to them safely.

Birthing with Eden was a slow, gentle experience. It was true the baby had her own timetable, and the contractions grew more painful with each crescendo and crash. Yet instead of relying on one great push, Joan listened to her body, went with its rhythms. She focused on the feeling of the water as it pulsed around her, heat trembling under her bottom and thighs. The girls knelt beside her and Eden, her co-conspirators, all those who could be trusted with kept secrets.

And when the big pain came, Joan screamed until she went raw. "Yes, that's right," Eden said, stroking her hair. "Let it out, my dear."

Joan heaved one final push past the ring of fire. The baby slid out, slippery as a fish, and Joan heard a first cry. Now she was moving up and up, drifting out of herself, seeing everything below her with new sight. She'd never felt closer to God.

SHE WOKE IN A DAZE, her brain swimming. No more dark walls closing in, no more tub. No more children, no more baby. The world around her was stark white. Machines hummed, the sound punctuated by soft beeps.

Joan blinked. A needle threaded through the inside of her elbow pinched her in an odd place. Her abdomen felt tender. Although she felt no pain, a kind of heavy damage held her down. She was alone.

When was the last time she'd been alone?

Her mouth went dry. She'd never been in a hospital, but she'd read about them in books. Most women gave birth there. Her cloudy thoughts said: *something went wrong.*

She didn't know how long she lay there dreaming until she heard the door. Bill trudged in, slamming it behind him, holding a paper cup —coffee, by the smell of it. "You're up," he said, monotone.

"What happened?" Her throat hurt.

"Lost the baby. Lost your womb." Redness surrounded Bill's eyes. "I suppose God has decided we should have no more children."

A rush of feeling went through Joan. *No more children.* She had to hold back her smile. It was like chains had broken.

But then she thought of her girl. She'd heard the lusty cry. Grief found a place to sit on her chest, and she struggled for breath. "How?"

"Rupture. You were bleeding out. The midwife called the Life-Flight." Bill circled her bed and sat beside her. "I wish you hadn't birthed with that woman. The church midwives have always treated you so kindly."

She'd labored in silence with twelve children. She'd been made to lie down, drink no water, speak no words. The church midwives stood around her, chanting, praying for her babies to be delivered unto God's world. They took the newborns and wrapped them, sprinkled them with water, passed them between each other's arms before Joan could even hold them. She'd ached to bring them to her chest, for them to lay across her skin.

Joan didn't have the strength to explain. "The baby. I heard her cry."

Bill's eyes went wide for a moment, but he didn't meet her gaze.

One of Joan's machines let out a mechanical cry. A set of scrubs-clad people ran into the room, pushing Bill out of the way. Joan felt herself dropping, fading out like maybe her daughter did.

## Judith

She watched the helicopter come. It was like nothing she'd seen in her life. A great swooping behemoth, lowering itself onto the only place with open ground: the yard right in front of their home. Her brothers and sisters woke screaming, running themselves to the windows, mouths agape. She hoped they didn't know that the woman on the stretcher being spirited across the grass was their mother.

Judith and her sisters had run back through the forest, Maribeth clutching the flashlight. Judith's heart was still pounding thirty minutes later, and sweat cooled on her brow.

The helicopter took to the air, its blades chopping like wind until it moved away from the house and into the dark. Judith laced her fingers behind her back in a sad imitation of prayer.

"Go back to sleep," she told the children, who still clamored at the windows. But even when they settled, the babies were waking. Judith heard them stirring upstairs, still lying in their cribs in their parents' room.

She crept inside, averting her eyes from the lump in the bed that was her father.

Judith was well-versed in her mother's ways. She grabbed a wrap and a ring sling from beside one crib. One baby went up on her back, and the second went on her front. This calmed them for a moment. It would be long enough to get downstairs and thaw bags of her mother's frozen milk.

The lump in the bed stirred. Her father snorted awake, sat up. "Joan?"

Judith blinked, her gaze fastened on the door. "Judy," she said.

"Oh." He smacked his lips together as if he were eating. "Where's your mother?"

There was a great bang from outside, like a gunshot. No, more like multiple gunshots, and the sizzle of fire in its aftermath.

The twins launched back into crying, and Judith closed her eyes. A heavy fatigue had settled over her, a combination of sleep deprivation and the kind of tiredness that lives in one's bones.

Bill launched out of bed and ran for the stairs, his steps like an elephant's. Judith wrinkled her nose at the smell that drifted past. It could only be described as old-man funk. And he was only in his boxers and a yellowed T-shirt that had once been white.

She didn't have time to think of much else. More screaming wafted up from downstairs. Judith willed herself to walk carefully, her brothers and sisters a higher priority than whatever was happening outside.

The flames came from far in the forest, at least a mile from the house. Judith blew out a breath. They would have time to escape—she hoped. Fires would spread, she knew, but she didn't know how fast or how far. She had not learned about these blazes in her homeschooling classes.

Bill was on the phone already. "We need the fire department. Yes, please, as fast as possible." He pointed at the younger ones, who crowded around Maribeth and Liliana. "Stay where you are!"

Judith didn't, though. She opened the front door and stepped outside. She still had her boots on from the trek across the mud—she'd tracked it all through the house in her haste to get the twins. The soil here was dry, though.

The light from the fire was everywhere. She clutched her sister to her chest and hiked her brother higher on her back. Miraculously, they quieted, maybe enthralled by the sight. Flames licked the sky.

Then Judith saw what she could only describe as a creature.

From her vantage point, it was small, but it must have been quite big to be seen from so far away. Its shape was vaguely human apart from the great wings that beat the air. She squinted. Were those horns protruding from its head? *The devil,* she thought as her breath caught in her throat.

Later, more helicopters arrived, coating the trees with some kind of flame retardant. Judith had gone back inside to prepare breakfast for her siblings. She already knew that the fire had subsided long before emergency services arrived.

JOAN RECOVERED in the hospital for four days. It would cost them so much, she knew. They didn't have insurance; the church would fund medical needs in a pinch, but they would owe thousands, and the church would not be able to cover that. Hospitals were worldly and to be avoided at all costs. Joan suspected she would be investigated for even birthing with Eden, and she hoped Eden would be safe from retribution.

But oh, it was heaven. No children at her feet, no tantrums, no demands. No one touched her, grabbed her, pulled her away from whatever she was doing. Eden brought her books, and the hospital brought her food. When she expressed her guilt, her nurse said, "Do not feel guilty, Mrs. Waite." The nurse's skin was brown, her scrubs magenta, and her coils of hair shook with her ardence. "You won't heal if you don't rest. Someone else will care for your children."

The church, her older daughters, Bill... She was not alone. And yet she was, and it was the best place she'd known.

Eden explained what had happened to the baby. Joan gawked. "That can't possibly be true," she said, palm over her heart. "You must be kidding."

Eden shook her head and reached for Joan's hand. Her palms were smooth and warm. "Hand to God. It was the strangest thing I've ever seen..." Eden's gaze drifted off. "But the most majestic. Joan, it was like the sky caught fire. She may be gone, but she's not dead. She's the most powerful creature in the Pinelands."

JOAN RETURNED TO HER HORDE. The children jumped around her, squealing and chattering. "Mother! I got an A on my math test!" "Mother, do you feel better?" "Mama, we missed you!"

Maribeth took her by the arm and seated her on the couch. Then she clapped her hands, and her siblings fell into line. "Listen, everyone. Mama is still not feeling well. We need to give her some space."

"I am happy to see you all." Joan's voice was scratchy. "I missed you."

Through the day, the older ones doted on her, bringing her tea and soup and making sure she was comfortable. The younger children curled up beside her, their sweet high voices telling her about their days, about everything Joan had missed. And the very youngest—Eli and her dear twins, who had weaned while she was gone—crawled carefully into her lap, guided by their sisters. Joan breathed in their sweet baby scents and hair.

Bill stalked around like a beast. He seemed to misunderstand what was happening in his own house. His wife rendered useless, her body no longer belonging to him. His children eager to please her instead of him. His power drained. And Joan reveled in it.

## Judith

Randy Henderson's truck idled in the Waites' driveway.

It was one of Judith's rare moments alone. She'd been standing in the room she shared with her oldest sisters, staring out the window. Everyone else was downstairs eating lunch, but Judith had told her father she didn't have an appetite. She'd said she would go upstairs and lie down. Was the funny feeling she had a premonition?

She rubbed the bridge of her nose. Lately, she'd been contemplating escape. She wanted to apply for college as far away from here as she could go. How would she even go, though, if she couldn't get online to fill out applications? How would she know if she had learned enough in homeschooling to cut it among the laypeople?

"Judith!" Her father's voice boomed from somewhere below. "Mr. Henderson is here."

She came down the stairs. Her stomach was churning now for real, her head pounding. She stopped on the landing. "I don't feel well."

There was too much noise. There was always too much noise. The kids gathered around the table slurping soup, chewing so loud she could hear it ricochet inside her ears.

Randy Henderson was not inside their house—Judith thanked God for that. Only family members were allowed inside Bill's sacred space. She didn't want to see that greasy hair again, those eyes that shimmered like slate. There was violence inside Randy, and she didn't want to be its object.

Bill advanced toward the staircase. "You will go out there."

Judith chewed her lip. It wasn't raining, but it was cold. Bill would be her chaperone, but where would they go?

She took a breath. Didn't have the energy to fight him. So she trudged down the stairs. At least Randy wouldn't be able to touch her. At least her father would stand there, beetle-browed, meaty arms crossing his chest. Judith got her coat and pushed on her earmuffs.

Randy Henderson looked hungry. She cringed at the thought of him devouring her.

The man turned off his truck and stepped down. Gave her father a big ole hearty handshake. "Well, sir, I thank you for coming," Bill said. "I'm happy for you to meet my daughter."

Randy raised one eyebrow. "We've met."

"I mean, formally," Bill said, but Judith figured Randy wasn't listening. His eyes were on her. She wore her traditional long dress, and the coat covered her body, but she felt his gaze. Removing those objects with his mind.

Bill's phone trilled. He stuck his hand in his pocket, pulled it out, frowned at the screen. "I have to take this. Judith, let me get your mother."

Judith's stomach clenched. "We need a chaperone."

"That's why I'm getting your mother," Bill said through gritted teeth.

"We can't be alone together," Judith said, trailing her father back into the house. "I can't be alone with him."

Bill waved a hand and started up the stairs.

Her mother stood at the sink, instructing her sisters through the pile of dishes left over from lunch. "What's going on, Judith?" she asked. "Mr. Henderson is here?"

"He's in the driveway. I need a chaperone." Judith leaned close, inhaled the scent of her mother's body wash and the tang of the lemon soap. "I want him to go away, Mother."

Joan nodded. She patted one of the girls on the shoulder and told her to finish up.

Randy's face looked stormy now as the two Waites approached, walking side by side. But he managed to conjure a pleasant tone. "Ladies. Mrs. Waite, nice to see you again."

"Thank you again for pulling us from that ditch." Joan beamed. The smile's falseness comforted Judith; her mother's closeness bolstered her. She felt safe.

"I have to say, it's the first time I noticed how lovely Judith is."

Joan wrapped an arm around Judith's shoulders. "She is special. Listen, Mr. Henderson—Judith isn't feeling well today, and it's not the best weather for courting. Can we please reschedule this visit? I'd hate for you to start off on the wrong foot."

The man licked his lips. "If you insist. But let's schedule something soon. You all come to town, maybe, and we sit inside?"

"That would be perfect," Joan said.

Randy hoisted himself back into the driver's seat. "You take care now."

When the truck had left the premises, Judith leaned into her mother, pushed her nose against her mother's arm. Joan rubbed her daughter's shoulders. And a cry rang out from the sky.

They both looked up. Judith gasped. It was the creature from the night they lost her baby sister. Joan shaded her eyes with her hand despite the lack of sun. "What is that?"

The dragon curled around itself, an elegant thing, not bothering to hide. Pointy horns fully on display, scaly wings beating. It moved leisurely, unhurried, cawing again before heading back into the trees.

THE STORIES BEGAN.

People in town whispered about the creature. Some had seen it circling above their houses, like Joan and Judith had. Others saw it on the ground, creeping between trees, poking its face out to reveal red eyes. No one dared to approach it, fearing death or even worse consequences. "The devil is here," preached their pastor, but the congregation could not confront it. For all they spoke of standing up to the devil, when faced with it, they retreated.

Joan wasn't scared. The creature visited her often and even seemed hesitant when they met on the ground. There was a resonance to their meetings, a purpose. Eventually Joan could hold out her hands, offering raw meat or bones, and the creature would take the food into the forest.

She welcomed those rumors. They gave people something to gossip about, leaving Joan and her children alone. Suspending judgment on the size of their family, on Joan's belly growing each year. There would be no more growing. Joan's body belonged to her alone. Even Bill avoided her, throwing himself into his work. Sometimes they didn't even go to church. The lights stayed on. Joan warded off the men who came courting, inventing mysterious illnesses involving boils and diseased private parts.

Joan spirited her girls to places with devices to access the Internet. Eden had a computer, though her connection was occasionally spotty.

They were at the library when Judith filled out her application for the Ohio State University. Judith was interested in the veterinary program, and though she felt her sciences weren't strong enough, she hoped to be admitted based on general studies. Maribeth and Liliana explored their options, combing through the homeschooling curricula to find subjects they could focus on.

She and Eden had become friends. Joan wanted to become a midwife, to give women options that served them. It wasn't easy, and Joan would have to take classes, but she was ready for it. Eden suggested she observe some births. Joan would sneak out in the middle of the night, sometimes at dawn or dusk—babies didn't wait for opportune times to arrive.

She was headed toward Eden's home when she saw the creature beside the lake. It was almost unrecognizable, curled in a tight ball, but Joan saw the horns peeking out. She didn't want to disturb it, but she couldn't take her eyes off it. It seemed so peaceful.

As if sensing Joan's presence, the creature lifted its head.

Joan took a step back as if she'd been pummeled. She dropped to her knees.

The next thing she knew, she felt soft breath on her cheeks. The creature had come to her, wrapping itself around her. Its leathery wings embraced her. She leaned back, felt its warm heart beating under the scales. Joan pressed herself to it and inhaled, pulling in that sweet baby scent.

"Please don't leave me," Joan said into its skin. "Please don't leave this place."

The creature stood, circled her one time, and she swore she saw it nod. It took to the sky with a graceful swoop of wind.

Eden stood at the door, watching. Her smile crooked as Joan stepped up to the porch. Joan could hear moans from inside, a woman getting ready for her life to change.

"You ready for a baby?" Eden asked as Joan came inside.

Joan grinned. "Always."

# MOTHWOMAN

Everyone's always talking about him like he's God. *Ooooh, Mothman, come fly me away.* He's got a museum. A festival. There's even that silver statue with his butt hanging out. People don't get it. What has he accomplished, really? Freaked out some people in a nuclear waste dump? Predicted the collapse of a bridge? He didn't even DO anything about it. *Mothman is my hero.* Bullshit.

I dumped that flat ass five years ago. He never did a thing to help me. I'd come home from working all day and he'd be sitting on the couch eating chips. Getting crumbs all over the $3000 furniture I had to finance at Value City. Great example for the mothkids. They'd be flying around throwing shit everywhere and he was messing around on his phone. I knew being a single mothmom would be hard, but at least I wouldn't have to look at him anymore.

And it is harder. I'm busting my ass every day. Working all day (car sales, what a grind), coming home to a mess to clean up, getting groceries, paying the bills. And he's in that nasty bachelor pad bringing swoony girls home every night so they can brag they boinked the Mothman. Meanwhile, no one even knows I exist.

And when he does take the kids, I don't have time to relax. I'm busy catching up on paperwork and the things I have to do around the house. He's the "fun dad" who gets to take the kids to Taco Bell and then out scaring people at night. All those little red eyes glowing in the dark.

Okay, I have to admit the kids are cute. They love me. But they also don't fucking listen. They sit in their rooms and watch YouTube. Or they're begging me for Roblox money, but they don't lift a wing to do any chores.

You know, I'm tired. All this shit and then I do it again every day. Even my wings hurt. Next time that deadbeat takes the kids, I'm setting time aside for self-care. Me time. I'm gonna head over to the bomb site and scare some teenagers out of losing their virginity. Yeah, that'll teach 'em. Fuck Mothman. I got this.

Ugh. It never ends. I need a therapist. And an assistant. I'll post some ads on care.com. Can't pay in money, but I can pay in smiles!

# MELONHEADS

My sister, like everyone, has a podcast. But she also claims to be a medium. I find that weird. Maybe because I still see her as a little girl dismembering Barbies. I don't recall any mystical experiences from our childhood, although she did bring home books on ESP and aliens from the library.

She calls me on a Saturday morning while I'm drinking coffee and doing my crossword. Theo is out at the gym. The window beside me is gorgeous and peaceful, looking out on our backyard blanketed with snow.

I pretend not to be annoyed when I answer. "Hey."

"Good morning, sister!"

She's always happy. I don't know what it's like to be in a mind like that. I don't even know what optimism is. "What's up?"

"I need you."

"Okay…" God, I hope she's not requesting money.

"I'm doing an episode on the Kirtland Melonheads."

I take a sip of my coffee. *Don't react. Radiate calm. Let her fill the silence.*

"C'mon, Sam. It won't be just us. My producer will be there. It'll be totally fine."

I grip the phone while I stare outside, trying to center myself. The wind is whipping a column of snow into the air. The chair feels like cement below me.

"Sam? Are you there?"

My voice cracks. "I'm here."

"Please. I can pay you for it. I'm finally starting to get ad revenue. Have you looked at my downloads lately? And I won't make you go on the mic if you don't want to, although it would be better if you did…"

I close my eyes. Why does coffee get cold so fast? I already need a warmer.

"Sam?"

"Let me think about it, okay?" I look down at the swirling liquid, shift in my chair. "I'll call you later."

I'M sure Lucy expected that I wouldn't call. She tries another tactic when I'm at work on Monday. It's nose to the grindstone every day in sales, but I check my phone at lunch to connect with Theo. His job is more flexible than mine, and he gets frustrated when he doesn't hear from me. I have a text from him and a text from Lucy.

I tap back a reply to Theo—*hope your day's going well, babe*—and then read her message. It's what I thought it would be. *I haven't heard back—are you okay? Have you thought about it?*

She always asks me if I'm okay. For someone who claims to be so intuitive, she is so dense. I sigh and reply. *I can't do it,* I type back. *Sorry.*

I learned early on that I have to set boundaries with my sister. She's the kind of person who wants to be in everyone's business. I'm sure that suits her well on her podcast since she gets to interview all kinds of woo-woo people. Besides, I need to focus on my salad. I usually have to force myself to eat because I'm always in work mode. I open my email and skim through it between bites.

The phone bleeps. Shit, I forgot to turn notifications off.

*Please. Don't you miss them?*

A memory twists inside me.

LUCY'S PRODUCER is named Gavin. He's cute. Young, with rich dark skin and an affable manner. We're in the studio, and he sticks out his hand. "Nice to meet you. I've heard so much about you."

People who know Lucy always say that. "It's nice to meet you too," I tell him.

The studio is warm, soundproof walls closing us in. They are made of blond wood, which opens the space and makes it feel less claustrophobic. There's a clear window that leads to the outside anteroom.

Lucy hasn't arrived yet. You have to tell her the time you want her there is an hour earlier than the time you actually want her there. Gavin must not have realized that yet.

"How long have you been Lucy's producer?"

He sits down in the chair beside one hanging microphone. "Not too long. She just started bringing in the funds to join up with my studio."

I'd looked up Lucy's downloads. She wasn't kidding. She's at over a million now. "I don't really follow her."

"One of her pods went viral. She did a deep dive into Bigfoot. Went up to the Michigan woods and everything. People love cryptids, man." Gavin shakes his head. "I'm sure she could have afforded her own producer. But we're a community here, and I think that appealed to her."

"So you have your podcast, then?" I glance around the room. It does seem like a nice setup. And cool that they can all share it.

"Nah. But I produce a lot of stuff and maintain the studio. Most of their fees go to me."

I nod slowly. "That's really cool." And I think I actually mean it.

Lucy's head appears in the window. She grins as she takes off her coat and hat. Gavin gets up to let her in.

"Oh my God, Sam. It is so nice to have you in the studio." Lucy leans down and hugs me, the lavender scent of her soap engulfing me. She's in a long skirt made of fabric patches and a blue cable-knit sweater. Her hair is wild and tangled, and as she sits in the chair beside me, she rubs her hands over it. "It's so cold out there!"

Gavin fixes her with a look. "Did you walk?"

"I mean, it's the most effective way to get here."

Apart from downtown, Kenmore is not really walkable. Lucy lives on a hill probably ten streets away in a tiny house she bought with some of her inheritance money. Considering she doesn't have a real job, though, she's always low on cash. Until now, I guess.

"Why didn't you tell me?" Gavin asks. "I could have picked you up."

She shakes her head, curls flying. "It's all good."

"At least let me take you home."

"I can do that." My offer pops out of the blue. I have no idea where it came from. Maybe instinct, from back when I used to take care of her, when our parents were busy with work and we were home alone. We didn't have a bad childhood, but like most nineties kids, we were latchkey.

Lucy gapes at me. "You would do that?"

"It's no problem." I cross my legs. "Well, we're all here."

Gavin rubs his hands together. "Great! Lucy, tell us what you're thinking. I want to have a game plan before we head out there."

"Okay. So Sam and I lived out there, not too far. We used to go down and play. That whole thing with the serial killer and the Mormons, though—that was creepy, so we stayed away for a bit. But we couldn't leave our friends for too long."

"That was the Lundgren case?" Gavin jumps up and turns some knobs on the audio rig. "We should be recording. I'll fix any issues in editing."

"Yeah, that place has super bad vibes." Lucy waves her hands in the air. "Joseph Smith actually cursed it when he left there for Utah. We weren't the greatest spot for a Mormon colony."

I know enough about Kirtland's history from our basic civics class, although we'd never covered the Lundgren case. It was too new. I remember checking through the paper every day after school, reading up on developments in the investigation.

"And the Melonheads—God, it's such a sad story."

"You have a personal connection to them," Gavin says, not as a question.

"Yeah." Lucy turns to me. "Sam, you want to say anything about it?"

*Not really.* I clear my throat. "They were kids. Experimented on. I wish... I wish they wouldn't call them that."

"Melonheads?" Gavin asks.

"Yeah." The anger comes out of me before I can stop it. "Part of the curse. That they were treated like that. Then left alone."

I squirm in my seat. There was this doctor—some said he was trying to save them, all those kids with swelling on the brain. But I don't believe it. Some say he injected them with even more fluid, or drained it out of their heads. This was in the forties. Not so primitive tools, but nothing like what we have today.

"And right by the Lundgren barn." Lucy shivers. "Who knew Joseph Smith had so much supernatural power?"

Jeffrey Lundgren killed an entire family after being deluded into thinking he was a Mormon prophet. It didn't feel like power to me. Only tragedy.

Gavin nods. "Good, good. This is great audio. Keep it going."

But my lips are sealed now. I can't let any more out. I'm too choked up thinking of Stephen.

After we complete the initial interview, Gavin takes me and Lucy to a coffee shop near the university. It's a Saturday afternoon. I'm assuming most students are partying and/or taking time off from studying. The people who are here are vibing, listening to headphones, chatting with friends, or tapping away at keyboards.

Lucy's addled as usual, jiggling her leg as she contemplates the menu.

"You don't have a usual order?" I ask. I generally don't like to bring up anything that might stir the pot, but if we have to stand here all day, I might spontaneously combust.

Lucy's eyes go wide. But Gavin laughs as he steps to the counter. "C'mon, Luce, or you're going to miss out on me paying."

That gets her in gear. I try to pay for my flat white, but Gavin waves me off too.

We find a table near a fogged window. I start thinking about what I'm going to do when I get home. There's a nice Mediterranean market nearby—I could grab some hummus and pita. I'm basic when it comes to shawarma too. Roast chicken tenderloins in the oven with spices and veggies, stuff them into wraps with Greek yogurt. Maybe Theo and I could play one of the murder mystery kits I like to buy. Fun, easy date night.

"Sam? Are you there?" Lucy snaps her fingers in front of my face.

I blink. "Sorry."

She rolls her eyes. Her turn to needle me.

Gavin clears his throat. "So I was saying we need to finalize plans for the visit."

"Visit?" I cough.

"Yeah..." The producer wraps his hands around his mug. "Lucy didn't tell you?"

Lucy lowers her head. "Guilty."

"You want to go there." There's a lump growing in my throat. "I don't know."

"Please? It'll be such great audio." Lucy clasps her hands and looks straight into my eyes. I can't help holding my gaze. In my mind she's still a child, all chubby cheeks and tangled curls. My little sister.

I look down into my coffee. My appetite has retreated. It might be Arby's for dinner.

Maybe it is time for me to see Stephen again. See how he's changed. See what his life is like now. If he'll tell me about it. If he understands.

Lucy's face drifts in front of me. I can't help it—the words spill from my mouth. "Aren't you worried about seeing them again?"

Her eyes flick to Gavin's. He maintains his calm. He must know some of the back story, then. How much has she told him?

"Yes," she says softly.

"You don't feel like you're exploiting them for cash?"

It comes out harsher than I intend, and she swallows. Gavin touches her arm. I feel like I can't get a breath, coffee and people tight around me, but then the front door jingles. A heavy wash of air gusts in as several giggling blond girls crash through.

"It's not about that," Gavin says. "This is a very personal story. Lucy's been focused on reporting her stories to build a platform. Now she has the opportunity to explore this part of her past." He lowers his voice. "Your past."

I don't have a reflection on that statement, so I sip my drink, which is growing colder by the moment. They're waiting for me to say something.

"You know," I say, "people make such valiant efforts to keep coffee warm. Fancy mugs, lids, all that. But look at this cup. No pretenses. This place knows it'll get cold. It doesn't pretend. Because eventually, they all get cold, right? And those paper cups say not to microwave them, but we have to if we want any sort of comfort, right?"

Both of them gape at me. "Does that mean you'll go?" Lucy asks.

I shrug. "Sure. Okay."

We work out the details for tomorrow. I'm not ready, but Gavin is itching to go, and I only have the weekend off. He will pick us both up at eight for the hour and a half drive to Kirtland.

I drive Lucy home as I promised. We don't say much. I can't speak for her, but my mind is full.

Theo is busy in the kitchen when I get back. So much for shawarma. Although I hadn't remembered to stop at the market anyway.

"How was your day? You saw your sister?" He kisses me as I pass him through our small galley kitchen. The smell of spiced beef wafts up, and I decide tacos will be just as delicious as anything I would have made.

I nod and head for my favorite spot by the window.

"You were there a long time."

"It wasn't too long. Just the time at the studio and then coffee after. I didn't really eat, though."

Theo grins and runs a hand back through his messy brown hair. "I got you covered."

He truly is a darling. If there is a bright side to death, I suppose it was that Theo worked at the funeral home where we buried my mother. I didn't mean to fall for a mortician's son, but it was one of those love-at-first-glance moments. He moved out here for me, for my job, as soul-sucking as it is. "But I'll be working for a new place now," he said when we'd first discussed marriage and moving in. "Almost unheard of in the industry—leaving a family institution. I might be able to start my own one day."

He's also seven years younger than me. Not jaded yet. But maybe it's just his demeanor. Theo is like a puppy, always happy to see you, always smiling. Gleeful even when confronting death. I don't know how I got so lucky. Especially after losing my first love. I often feel that I don't deserve Theo.

"You don't know how much I appreciate it, sweetie." I sit at the table and watch him work. Somewhere on the other side of our house, the sun is setting, and the yard behind me grows dark.

After we eat, I break out one of the mystery games. It takes us an hour or so to solve it, and then I settle in front of the TV for some zoning-out time. I love lazing about on a Saturday night, content to remain inside while the rest of the world has a social life. I might scroll through Instagram or do a puzzle on my phone.

Theo returns from the kitchen with two cold glasses of white wine. *So freaking lucky,* I say to myself as I accept it.

"How did it all go?" Theo fits his long frame into the armchair by the window, his knees in the air. He likes to pretzel himself that way, and I have no complaints. "You're going to be on a podcast. How crazy."

"Yeah." My phone slips from my lap as I cradle the wineglass. "It was weird."

"How so?"

"They want me to go to Kirtland with them."

Theo's family funeral home is there, so he understands. He whistles. "Damn."

"Yeah, I mean… it's not like going up to visit your family." Though I'm not a huge fan of that either, but Theo doesn't have to know that.

"Do you want me to come with you?"

I get a striking sense that he should not be there. That I have to face this, even if Gavin and Lucy are with me. Especially that Lucy will be with me. My sweet, sunny husband does not need to see my dark side.

"I'm okay. I'll be with Lucy and her producer. I can't imagine it will be long. Do you want me to say hello to your parents while I'm there?"

Theo laughs. "That's not necessary. Well, I understand. You can tell me all about it when you get home."

I put the wine down, get up, and throw my arms around him. He hugs me tight.

It's me, Gavin, and Lucy cruising down Route 90 in a silver Honda Accord. I've picked the skin at my thumb so much it's bleeding. My anxiety is spiky, a living thing pushing adrenaline through me. I shouldn't be like this—we're not going to see anyone or anything. All this is an exercise in futility. They don't like to be out during the day, and the sun is so bright.

Lucy has charmed one of the nearby farm owners into letting us park in their driveway. "We'll walk and talk," she says, beckoning us to the street.

"There aren't any sidewalks," Gavin says. He's setting up his recording equipment, now in a complicated traveling rig.

Lucy and I look at each other, and we both laugh.

"You haven't spent enough time in the country, have you?" She jostles Gavin's arm.

"Hey!" He tips back on his heels. "Watch the technology."

"We will be walking in the road," I add. "That's how we do it."

"Got that on tape," Gavin says, but he looks nervous as we set out onto the street.

Ahead of us, Lucy kicks rocks with her clompy Doc Martens. She has on a pair of holey jeans and a flowing, off-the-shoulder neon shirt under her unzipped winter jacket. "Um, how is this going to sound on audio?" I ask Gavin, indicating my sister's noise creation.

"Ambiance," he says. "She's setting the scene for her voiceover."

"I can hear you!" Lucy calls over her back. "I actually know what I'm doing, Sam." She tromps harder.

I look at the concrete. Cars fly by, swerving wide to avoid us. We're hugging the ditch beside the small farms and wooded areas, and the smell of soil is all too familiar. Earthy and wild, a hundred different forms of life flourishing below us.

Lucy takes a bank into a long driveway. We've gone past the Lundgren land and the church. "There's only one way to get in the forest," she says.

Gavin moves closer to the mic. "Say it again."

"There's only ONE way to get in the FOREST!"

I chuckle.

"Hey, sister, your glass facade is breaking." Lucy points at me. "Do you actually think I'm funny? Wait, now that I have gainful employment, it's different, right?"

Any humor I had in me vanishes. I watch her step back up to lead us, curls bouncing against her pink blouse.

The woods grow deeper. My breath hitches.

Even though the sun is high, the canopy of trees blocks the light. And it's cold, oh so cold. It feels darker here, the soil more earthy, plants everywhere. A squirrel sweeps by. Ants and spiders and every variety of beetle crawl under desiccated logs.

*Slugs,* I think. Stephen loved them. Especially when we were very young, seven or eight maybe. He would overturn every log he could find, slipping them out and staring in awe at his slimy fingers.

"Gross," I'd say. "You're gonna wash your hands, right?"

He'd grin and push his palm into my face. Then I'd screech as he chased me, threatening me with his dirty mitts.

Lucy was little then. I'm not sure she even went with me to the woods that long ago. Mom would have kept my sister by her side, never letting her out of her sight. Lucy was Mom's favorite. Lucy was there when Mom died.

Now Gavin is recording our footsteps as we press down the leaves underfoot. In the hush of the woods, Lucy begins her narration.

"This is where it began." She does sound professional. There must be a reason people subscribe to her, I suppose. "I'm here with Gavin—my producer, if you're new to the pod—and my sister, Samantha. You heard from her earlier in the studio."

Gavin elbows me. It's the only part of him free as he records from the rig.

"Hi," I say to the mic. "It's me. Sam."

Lucy lifts her chin.

"We're here in the forest where the two of us liked to play. Down the road from the site of the Lundgren murders. Our house was—" Lucy points, then laughs. "Sometimes I forget it's just audio. We're behind our old house."

I crane my neck in that direction. "Is it still there?"

"We'll have to drive by on our way, but I think it was razed for a McMansion." She twists her lips. "I'm sure our friends were not happy about that."

I don't think they care. Stephen was never interested in the outside world. He said they had everything they needed, and that was enough.

"But what about the cabins?" I say the last thing I'm thinking and stop suddenly. Lucy and Gavin stop too, and Lucy puts a hand to her mouth. "Aren't they the reason we're here?"

"They were maybe a mile back on the land. So if we're too far away to see the house, but we're too far away to see them, we must be in the middle."

The flutters are back in my stomach. "But what if they were torn down too?"

Lucy doesn't respond. She just sets her chin and marches off toward the spot.

THIS IS HOW I KNOW: we arrive at a clearing. It is in the precise place where the cabins were. There is a tree with initials carved into it like lovers do. S&S, because Stephen doesn't have a last name. *Didn't.*

Lucy stalks alongside the tree, noticing the marks. "Sam. Did you do this?"

I hesitate.

She shakes her curls. "My sister is refusing to speak," she tells the mic. Gavin looks like he's trying to become part of the forest.

What can I say? The cabins are gone. Our friends are gone. Sure, their heads were swollen. They were not beautiful. But they were kids like us. With kids' dreams and kids' resourcefulness and kids' hearts.

"This is where they lived," I say in a strangled voice.

Lucy and Gavin turn to look at me.

"Don't call them the Melonheads," I tell the mic. "They had names. Stephen. Jane. Henrietta, Wallace, Bridie. They had people who loved them, people who went into town and brought them provisions so no one in the real world would see them. Someone took this all away from the place where we met."

My voice is getting stronger. Lucy and Gavin don't jump in.

"If their houses were torn down, where did they go?" I put my face in my hand and shake my head. "Did they find someplace else to live? Or did they just die? Were the cabins razed with them still inside? Did someone think they deserved to die because they were ugly?"

Lucy gasps. "That doesn't sound nice, Sam."

"It's not nice, but it's true!" I whip toward Lucy as a wave of my brown hair hits my cheek. "That's why they couldn't go out in public, right? They'd be seen as strange. Cryptic. Like, isn't that what a cryptid is? A fairy tale—but they were real. *Are* real."

My chest is heaving. I go up to the tree and gently move Lucy out of the way so I can look at the engraving. Stephen had used his Swiss army knife to gently carve the bark off. I remember standing next to him, marveling at the skill he had, inhaling the sweet smell of the flowers surrounding us. His mother's garden. Now those flowers are consumed by weeds.

"And I left him here," I say softly, not loud enough for the mic to pick up. "Because..."

"Middle school," Lucy says frankly. "Gavin, can you cut the audio?"

I kneel and feel that wet earth on my knees. Shiver as I pull my fleece coat tighter around my neck. I'm covered in guilt.

Lucy touches my shoulder. "It's okay, Sam. Tweens are shallow. It wasn't cool to hang out with quote-unquote 'freaks.'"

"But they weren't! At least..." I get up, holding the tree for balance. "They weren't to us. And I still left them."

"We all had to, in the end. They weren't part of the real world. And one day, we all had to become adults." Lucy pauses. "Even me."

"I THINK WE HAVE ENOUGH," Gavin says as we trudge back toward the car. It's quiet and getting colder. We've been walking for so long that my feet feel like ice blocks.

"Yeah, plenty," Lucy says. "I'm sad, though. This doesn't fit with my vision."

We reach the car, and she climbs into the back seat. I sit in the front and turn on the seat warmer. Gavin packs the trunk and then joins us, ready to return to the freeway.

"What's your vision?" I ask once we are fully ensconced.

She sighs. "I was hoping to see them."

I turn around to look at her. "Did you think they would even come out?"

Lucy is silent for a minute, and all I hear is the hum of the heater. "They would for you," she says finally. Gavin exits onto the highway, the rest of our path straightforward.

We don't say much on the way back, but I tell Lucy I'll call her before I leave the car.

Theo is waiting. He's already been to the gym. His rotation doesn't include "leg day," but he does have a system. Weights on Tuesday and Thursdays. Runs on Saturdays and Mondays.

"Hey!" He puts down his book and jumps up to take my coat. "How did it go?"

Sometimes his energy is too much for me. I try not to buckle, to rain on his goofy and sweet parade, but this time I can't hold it in. I collapse against his chest and let myself cry. He runs his hand over my head. Sometimes this is the way we communicate, me in my feelings, him holding me until I have the strength to start over.

I sniffle and move back. He holds me at arm's length, concern in his expression. His beautiful face all on display, and me wondering again how I got so lucky.

~

THE PODCAST GOES LIVE the following Wednesday. I listen to it with my headphones on at work. It's not too bad, actually. I thought I would sound like a Muppet, but the sound gear enriches my voice. I almost sound professional. Like Lucy.

My coworkers clap or smile as they walk by my cube. Everyone has heard it. For a few days, I'm a semi-celebrity. But the news cycle is what it is, and by Friday they are on to Taylor Swift's appearance at a football game.

I figure that's the end. I'm rattled, though. As I'm walking to the parking deck on Friday, one of my coworkers yells out, "TGIF, right?" The words echo from the ceiling, and I think, *I'm such a fucking cliche.*

Yes, I get home to the most amazing man. Our life is nearly perfect. Especially these weekends, where his only obligation is to his gym, and mine is to the crossword puzzle. And the coffee has its obligation to me.

But what does perfect mean if something is missing?

Theo usually returns about half an hour after I get home. It gives me time to unwind before we decide what to do for the evening. I loosen the button on my skirt and slump into the chair, then check my personal email on my phone.

There's one that says "no subject" and comes from a mysterious address. I am sure it is spam and am on the way to delete it when I see words in the preview text.

*It's Stephen. I heard your podcast.*

That fluttering is back. But I can't delete it now even if it is someone scamming me. I open it to find a link to YouTube. An unlisted video, an all-dark space. I press play.

His voice is the same, except richer now that he's older. *We're* older.

"Sam, hi." The lights are off in the room he sits in. I can only see the outline of his head and movement around his fingers as he twitches. "I thought I should say this to you instead of writing it out. I don't know if you will actually hear it, but I thought I would try."

*Maybe you should have put a subject in the email.* I keep watching.

"It's nice that you were worried about us. We're OK, though. We moved off the land before they came to destroy the place. You're right, your house is gone, and there's a fancy one there now. I guess they didn't want those old structures to junk up their backyard. Even if no one could see them."

There's a note of disgust in his voice. He continues.

"You know Gretchen? She got us a place. It was the bunch of us, all on top of each other in this tiny apartment, but it worked okay. Because one by one, we started to leave. With more opportunities online, we started to get our degrees. And we found people we could trust with our secrets. I'm a doctor now, running lab tests on kids with hydroencephaly." He laughs dryly. "Ironic, huh? But I'm not injecting fluids into them. Trying to hurt them. I'm making things better. Making it so kids like us don't have to suffer like we did."

I let out a breath. Stephen's doing things that matter while I'm cold-calling and hustling for commission. "I really did fail," I murmur to the screen.

Stephen's tone softens, and I know he's going to bring it up. "I get why you left," he says. "We don't have to keep reliving it. I can tell you feel guilty. But I also know you're happy now. And before you get creeped out, remember we're not in the woods anymore. Google exists."

I shake my head. He doesn't know. He really doesn't.

"Anyway. You have my email. Reach out sometime. I'd love to talk."

A light flicks on, and I can see him—all of him. His bloated head, yes, but also his face. His eyes that always reflected so much hope. Even the skin of his cheeks is the same. Pale, flushed, and soft.

"Stevie? You in there?" A woman steps into the room. I catch a quick glimpse of her before Stephen cuts the camera off. She looks a bit like me.

"Hey babe!" Theo bursts in, the screen door clattering. "What are you watching?"

My mouth is dry. I look up at him, look down at the phone. I hold it all in my hands: my Lucy, my Stephen, all the love I pushed away, traded for this.

Theo hops over my legs and nestles beside me on the couch. "Anything good?"

I manage a smile. "I'll show you."

# APPENDIX

**Story Origins**

ost of my sources were from the Internet and personal experience; I did look at a few books about the Lake Erie Monsters. (I know, bad librarian, but this is fiction, right?)

## *"I Loved the Mothman"*

I mentioned the context of this story in the introduction. It appears in *Passageways: Mythos* (Writing Bloc, 2023) and was the genesis of all the stories.

## *"Greg from Accounting"*

This story came about because my coworker Mark had suggested I write about the Mongolian death worm. I had never heard of this cryptid, so of course I had to research it. Reminiscent of monsters in Frank Herbert's *Dune,* the death worm's legend was first recorded in America by a paleontologist visiting Mongolia, but the story had circled in that country for much longer. It is called *olgoi-khorkhoi* (large intestine worm) there. Like the Mothman and the sandhill crane, the death worm was probably an animal, possibly the Tartar sand boa.

Mark was instrumental in coming up with the plot; I think he'll be surprised that I actually wrote it. In the special edition of this book, Mark's illustration appears with this story.


## "Sassy"

Transformation is a strong theme in this book. Sasquatch/Bigfoot is possibly the most famous cryptid, and I knew that anything I wrote would have to be unique. I liked the idea of a girl embracing her true identity even though it went against who her friends thought she was.


## "The Portrait of Indrid Cold"

I found out about Indrid Cold when I was looking through lists of cryptids I might write about. This creepy man simply stands, stares, and smiles at people, either close up or far away. It reminded me of the monsters in *Buffy the Vampire Slayer's* masterful episode, "Hush." Those smiling creatures take away everyone's voices so they can't scream for help when the monsters take them. Our characters don't lose their voices, but the people Cold takes do. I also (obviously) wanted to cross-reference this man with Oscar Wilde's *The Portrait of Dorian Grey,* because there had to be a reason the cryptid could continue existing without being destroyed. Mentioned in the 2002 film *The Mothman Prophecies,* it's possible this character could be connected to the Mothman as well, because its first sighting was in West Virginia near Parkersburg. My characters' fate is different from that of the man who appeared to Woodrow Derenberger, the first person to spot Indrid Cold. Derenberger faced public criticism, and his wife eventually left him. I liked the idea of giving Bernie and his friends a happier ending.

### "The Little Monster"

I couldn't write a book about cryptids without including Lake Erie Larry and Bessie. Bessie is well-known as the monster who inhabits the lake, but she's also been described as Lake Erie Larry. The Cleveland Monsters hockey team was even once called the Lake Erie Monsters. The monsters are supposed to be much more frightening, more like sea serpents, but I wanted to portray a sweeter story based on *The Little Mermaid.* I also split Bessie/Lake Erie Larry into two cryptids so they could play off each other.

### "Exit Through the Gift Shop"

This story was inspired by a day at the zoo with my family. I had forgotten how many young families come to the zoo because, well, there isn't much to do when you have little kids. As I watched the parents struggle, my empathy kicked in, and I remembered how hard that age was. Motherhood is a strong theme in many of these stories also, and Daphne arrived in my mind like one of the women I saw at the zoo that day. I wanted her to feel some kind of freedom in the end, even if it was only for a few hours.

### "Clearance Hamster"

My husband will often say that clearance racks are "the stuff that no one wants." We were at the pet store one day, and he speculated that there might be a poor hamster who no one wanted. I thought... what if that hamster were a cryptid? I love the jackalope because it is so fickle; it can be destructive one moment and protective the next. It can also sing. With the jackalope, Katy realizes that she can move on from her bad relationship and trust her allies.

*"Loveland Frog and Loveland Toad are Friends"*

As a child, I loved Frog and Toad, the iconic characters created by Arnold Lobel. The Loveland Frog is a creature from Loveland, Ohio, spotted in the fifties by a late-night traveler. A police officer in the seventies, Ray Shockey, later encountered the giant frog in his own headlights. I created an origin story for the Loveland Frog and gave him a friend. I endeavored to write the story in Lobel's style.

*"Curves"*

I have to admit that this story is close to my own experience. I've always hated the way I look, and Jessie is a strong representation of myself. It would be so nice to transform into something that held power but did not need to justify itself with its looks.

*"Greener Grass"*

My colleague Kaytalin mentioned that there were some TikTok videos where people were saying the Fresno Nightcrawlers stole their wallets. I was thinking of the Nightcrawlers as scams and schemers, and I merged this with a traveling salesperson who came to my house and tried to sell me a lawn service. I actually paid for the lawn service for several years before canceling it, even though it did nothing for my yard. I used the YouTube format because Greg and Joshua's voices were so vivid in my mind; I felt that writing that section in prose would take away from their interactions and dialogue.

*"Devil Thirteen"*

This was a tough one. I had read the legend of an eighteenth-century woman who had twelve children before her thirteenth turned into a monster. "Mother Leeds" cursed her thirteenth child, but I wanted Joan's child to be more of a savior, especially because Bill was so controlling and cruel. I don't know where the idea of the church/cult came from; I'd read the book about the famous Duggar family, so I could have picked up inspiration from that. Mother Leeds seemed to feel hampered by her many children, and Joan wouldn't have chosen this life if she were free—yet she loves those children unconditionally.

### *"Mothwoman"*

After writing "I Loved the Mothman," I learned that many stories of falling in love with the Mothman already exist. I thought I was doing something new! I started thinking about what would happen to Mothman's partner if he was always out falling in love with people. This story came quickly and was a product of feminine rage. Rest assured, though, that my husband is not the partner Mothman is.

### *"Melonheads"*

I wrote about this story in the introduction also; when I learned about the Kirtland Melonheads, I had to investigate them because I know Kirtland. I couldn't believe how the story dovetailed with the Lundgren murders and the curse of Joseph Smith. The Melonheads were rumored to have come from an evil doctor who induced hydrocephalus —water on the brain—in children, and they also existed because of Smith's curse. The Melonheads also lived near the property where Jeffrey Lundgren killed and buried the Avery family in 1989.

# ACKNOWLEDGMENTS

Thank you to the Duskbound team. My books wouldn't exist without you. Kaytalin Platt is our cover designer and social media maven; Gino Finocchiaro is our intrepid formatter and handles all things book design. Mike X Welch is our author wrangler. Aly Welch rounds out the team with her expertise in developmental editing and proofreading. Everyone contributes to proofreading and developmental editing too, and they are all outstanding writers on top of all that talent. (I'm just the lowly line editor.) I am in awe of them every time we release a book.

Master genealogist and history expert Ashley Sroka helped me to find information on Robert L. Smith, the professor mentioned in "I Loved the Mothman." She is a coworker and a great friend also.

If you don't hold the special edition in your hands, you should get one! These talented folks contributed their artwork to the special edition paperback and the hardcover. A special thank you to Alex Holmes, Ryan Sandy, Kayla Kochis, Alex O'Sullivan, Mark Simon, Kaytalin Platt, and Clara Madsen.

I would be remiss if I didn't thank the friends and writers' groups who listen to my nonsense. Special thanks to Jill Liepins, Alex Smith, Lori Holmes, Julie Anne Hatcher, L.A. McGinnis, Danielle Haas, Kathryn Long, Jane Ann Turzillo, Chelsea Banning and the Ohio Dragon Writers, Amanda Flower, Shellie Arnold, Kathryn Feeley, and Jessica Madsen.

As always, thank you to my family; they always support me. Henry, the sweetest kid in the world, and Oliver, Devil Two in my family. Ed Dubiel, whose own talent surpasses the average bear and more. My sister, Jamie Stevenson, is always there for me and reads everything I write. I love you!